Remy Bake It Up To You

Shannon Massey

Copyright © 2024 Shannon Massey

All rights reserved.

ISBN:
979-8-89504-235-9

Thank you to my family and friends!

(Mom: this book is safe for you to read there are no horror shenanigans haha)

Kids: you're amazing, I'm so glad I get to be your mom. I love you to infinity!

Students: Always remember: you're smart, you're capable, and you can do this. I believe in you :)

This book wouldn't have been possible without the help of:

Parasite_Z, thank you for the amazing cover art!
Find their art here: https://vgen.co/parasite_z

Bex thank you for your help with Remy!

Candace, thank you so much for your help with the cover design!
Find more about Candace's author services here:
https://foxglovefiction.com/author-services/

Kayla, thank you for your help with Amelia and her family!
Find her sensitivity/authenticity reader services here:
https://www.fiverr.com/s/6YXLRZN

Yo thank you for your help with edits.

Thank you so much for choosing to spend time with Remy and Amelia! This started as a short story for a queer holiday anthology that never got off the ground. I couldn't let Remy and Amelia stay on my laptop though so I expanded the story and here we are :)

As a single mom, I want to thank you for buying my book. Book sales help me do things like buy groceries and pay school fees.

CW: Remy is a trauma ball that hides behind snark, sexual innuendos, and charm which may be triggering for some people. Mention of workplace trauma (verbal/physical abuse in kitchens), mention of childhood trauma (verbal/emotional/physical abuse some linked to weight and bullying), mention of unhealthy eating habits bordering on an eating disorder (thinking about purging, mention of dieting), swearing, drinking, a character has a panic attack, a character has a near death experience, recovering from hypothermia. Characters stranded in a diner in a snowstorm, Amelia's mom has ovarian cancer.

Remy is a multi-racial British character, since she's the POV character the book is in UK English vs US English :)

Happy reading!

After you read if you can take two minutes to leave a rating or review, I'd appreciate it :)

1

The road is quite straight, stretching past the end of the world. Snow started at half three, as Remy rushed from the airport and into the last rental in whatever godforsaken state she was stuck in. She can't be stuck in the US for Christmas; her younger sister, Violet, had a baby. Vie's one of those hipsters that wants the child to choose its own gender. Of course adults can choose whatever pronoun and gender they want. However, an infant? Remy thinks the notion is a load of shite, but can't wait to watch her family fumble as they try to appease their favourite.

She bought a bottle of cheap American whiskey and a large can of what they call beer before leaving town and following her satnav towards the next airport. Typically, she'd never drink drive but with the weather she needs to concentrate and drinking helps her focus, so this should make things better instead of everything worse?

There are two radio stations to choose from: one that rages on hellfire and brimstone, the other obnoxiously twangy with grown men crying about their trucks and dogs. With no phone service, she can't play Tidal, she should have upgraded to premium. She's building a new playlist that's almost as good as her 'fancy a shag?' list. American women love it and think she's so clever. If only she could meet someone, anyone, that sees through her nonsense and calls her on it.

The snow grows heavier, causing the road to become increasingly difficult to see and stay on. Remy wrestles with the steering wheel of the car as it careens along the road. Snow piles up, trying to push the car back and hold it where it rolls. Over the past hour, the snow shifted from fun powder that dances about snow globes to horrid sheets blanketing everything. Remy slows to a crawl, she hasn't seen a living soul or building in ages.

"Please don't let me die in the fucking armpit of this country," Remy whispers as she lights a cigarette.

The blankets of snow get heavier and car wipers race frantically to keep up. Sliding down the road with her hazards flashing, an abandoned pickup pops out of nowhere. Remy swerves, Marlboro clenched between her teeth. She can't wait to get home and get real cigarettes again. American cigarettes make her lungs feel like they're being cut by glass.

The car spins doughnuts, like the teacup ride at Disneyland Paris when she was five.

"Fuck, fuck, fuck!" Remy repeats, keeping her cigarette clenched between her teeth.

Though she rights the car, it hits a ditch; the front slams into a snowdrift. The airbag deploys, cigarette burning a hole through it and the car stalls and dies.

Remy does a quick check for all her parts and pieces. Thankfully, they're all where they should be. She didn't spill the beer or lose the whiskey flask. First she finishes the beer, then lights another cigarette before undertaking the daunting task of getting out of the car. With the front doors buried, Remy kicks at the rear driver door until she can squeeze out. She's dazed but has the sense to grab her handbag, whiskey, and phone.

Unfortunately, the phone has no signal. However, faint tracks move up the road, so she follows them. Remy's ballet pumps are for a plane, not trekking through a metre of snow. Bitter cold stabs through to her bones before the hazard lights have even disappeared into the blankets of snow she pushes through. The cigarette drops from chattering teeth, and frigid air makes each breath hurt. Luckily, the whiskey helps to warm her, but hurts to swallow, US whiskey is so harsh. Remy's linen suit worked for the final meeting in LA that morning but does nothing for her now.

Her body is a block of ice, and she can't remember where she's going, but hopes to lie down when she gets there. The snow could wrap around her like a blanket.

Oh, like a mattress; Remy lies down, a nap won't hurt. The hum of the angel's song trumpets above the snow. The song gets louder, she won't be able to sleep with all the racket.

Floating is such a strange feeling.

Oddly, there are no Christmas decorations. Remy stands in knee's deep snow, trying to remember the last time she saw this much on the family estate. Snow flutters inside and outside the house. Everyone frozen in place, like ice statues. The baby suckles on a bottle filled with snow. Mother is talking with Helga and Viktor. Father is in his study smoking a pipe made of ice. Everything fractured and disjointed.

The ice begins to melt and crack. One by one the members of the family shatter into a million pieces. Remy sinks deeper into the snow. No matter how hard she wants to struggle she's made of ice too. As if in slow motion, pieces crack and fall off her.

2

Remy's pieces are where they're supposed to be; yet, that supposed to be is on a hard floor with a doughy bottle blonde on top of her. They're both in bra and knickers under a mound of musty blankets. At least it isn't the same weight that haunts her nightmares? The doughy blonde's body seems to envelop Remy, the sensation sending waves of panic and nausea through her.

"Ruby, she's comin' round!" the woman on top of Remy shouts then smiles down at Remy. "Relax, I ain't gettin' fresh, just tryna getchya thawed, hypothermia's skin't'skin."

Remy wants to say something smart about the unintelligible rubbish spewing from the woman's mouth. But it's as if she's swimming through muck, her mind and body aren't reacting as they should. "Hm?"

Everything fades back out.

The kitchen is ice, everyone frozen.

"What the fuck is this?! I wouldn't feed it to alley rats."

Chef throws a pie at Remy, it flies at her in slow motion shattering into millions of icicles; the shards cut her and cause her to shatter.

Remy can't open her eyes. At least she doesn't feel the doughy woman on her anymore; the weight is lighter, possibly a blanket?

"Sure you got this, Amelia?"

"Yes, go, get the house put together. I'll stay here with her, we shouldn't move her just yet."

Remy hides in the classroom wardrobe from her Luckley classmates trying to smother her tears. Everything is snow and ice, and she can't move, she's frozen too.

"Here, Piggy, Piggy, Piggy," echoes down the halls.

"Can't hide forever, I saw you eye me up! Gonna make you squeal,"

Remy wants to run, needs to get away before they catch up. There's never anywhere *to* run, though.

"Shhhh, you're okay, you're safe," someone murmurs.

Hot tears rush down Remy's cheeks. "Don't Gemma," she forces out.

"Shhh, you're safe, Gemma isn't here," she's reassured again.

Remy is on the family estate, but it's also the kitchen and Luckley? With no way to escape, she keeps trying to run but she's frozen, each step pulls another piece off of her. Shattering bit by bit as plates hit her.

"Piggy, have another cake." Remy's choking on the snow crumbs being forced in her mouth by Charlotte while Gemma pins her to the chair.

"If you insist on being a disgusting cow, at least in the kitchen no one has to look at you," Mother says, studying the scale disapprovingly.

"This isn't dessert, it's a fucking disaster you worthless cunt!" The finished dessert plate hits Remy and she shatters.

Remy tries to scramble away but moving is hard, she's sore. She gets her arms up, at least she can protect her head.

"Hey, hey, you're safe, you're okay,"

Remy can't shake the ice from the dreams or the snow in her mouth, she gags coughing.

"Shhhh, you're okay, let's take some deep breaths,"

Soft, callused hands are holding Remy's, gently rubbing her wrists. She's trying to breathe with the petite woman with freckled brown skin, large doe eyes, and corkscrew curls sitting in front of her. Wearing what looks like a borrowed tracksuit that hangs off her. With the sleeves rolled up and resting just above her delicate wrists.

"There you go, you're safe, you're at Ruby's Diner. I'm Amelia Haskins."

"Remy... Kensington." It takes effort to make her mouth form around the two words and to push them out.

Amelia smiles warmly, causing slight dimples to form at the corners of her mouth. "You've had us worried, Remy. Let's take things slow, okay?"

Remy is also in a borrowed tracksuit that is too big for her, lying on the floor of a kitchen in front of the ovens under musty blankets.

"There's another woman?" Remy says, unsure if there actually was, or if that was a dream.

Amelia nods. "Ruby and Georgia got stuck back in the house when they went to get the guest rooms set up. It's just you and me here."

Remy is having trouble staying awake. "I'm tired," she mumbles.

"You had something pretty big happen. If you need to rest you can, I'll be right here, you're safe, no one can hurt you."

When Remy wakes in a dead panic, she's alone in the kitchen. She scrambles out front, running from things she can never escape. The other woman sits with a blanket around her shoulders at the counter, reading.

She looks up with a warm smile. "Hey, you're okay Remy, you're safe, I'm Amelia, you're in Ruby's Diner."

Remy isn't sure about that, she can't shake the nightmares. Everything was ice, everything was—she needs to get ahold of herself.

"Want to sit and we can breathe together?"

Remy slumps at the counter next to Amelia. "I have nightmares," she manages.

"Want to talk about them?" Amelia asks.

Remy shakes her head slightly. She's trying to take deep breaths and listen to Amelia count while she rubs Remy's wrists.

"There you go, we'll just take a few more then I can get you something warm to drink. You hungry?"

Remy shakes her head, she can't eat after what Gemma and Charlotte were doing in the dream, she wants to vomit, but that always helps. Perhaps she'll find the loo so she can regain some control.

"Here, take this, I doctored it the right way, it's almost tolerable," Amelia says, pushing a steaming coffee mug over to Remy. She stands, shifting her blanket off her slight shoulders and onto Remy's. Even standing, she's small as she goes around the counter and leans down to grab another mug from a rickety silver shelf. "Had us worried, how are you feeling?" Amelia asks over her shoulder.

Remy shakes her head and shrugs with a deep breath, pushing it out. "I should get back on the road, need to get home."

"We're not going anywhere, sorry," Amelia says, gesturing

behind Remy. "Where's home?"

Remy glances back, snow drifts pile against the doors and windows. "West London. My sister had a baby, I want to meet the bugger."

"Understandable. I know you probably hate hearing it but I love your accent," Amelia says, sitting back down next to Remy with another mug of coffee.

"I'm not the one with an accent, you are," she responds, trying to flash a disarming smirk.

Amelia laughs. "That's funny, ya know I'd never thought about it like that. How'd you end up here?"

"Suppose a red pickup? I swerved to miss it."

A mortified look flickers over Amelia's perfect, heart-shaped face. "On no, was I the reason you ran off the road?"

Remy nods and takes a sip of the coffee. The warmth helps chase away the phantoms from the nightmares and the chill that won't seem to leave.

"I'm so sorry!" Amelia says, expressive face twisted with remorse. "Are you really okay?"

Remy nods. "I'm no longer a human ice lolly and I can think a bit more clearly." She's a bit wobbly, like she had a few too many, but it's not awful.

"Good, that's good. I know you aren't hungry, but eating something will help. Can I fix you up a bowl of chilli?"

Remy looks back at the windows and doors, the walls are closing in. "Perhaps I'll do a bit of baking? I don't like being stuck or idle."

"Okay, we'll want to take things slow, you're still recovering. Why don't we see what you have to work with while I fix us a couple of plates?"

Remy nods and slowly stands taking a second to find her footing before following Amelia back towards the kitchen.

3

Remy follows Amelia into the kitchen, trying and failing to not ogle Amelia as she walks.

Amelia glances back over her shoulder. "Eyes up, Kensington."

Remy laughs. "I was just thinking I need to stop watching you walk. I'm not eyeing you up, I assure you."

Amelia smiles. "Mm-hmm."

"Why don't you take care of the chilli? I'll look to see what goodies I can make," Remy says. Shifting into kitchen mode helps her shake away the fuzz still hanging on.

Amelia moves over to the chilli, strides more purposeful, teasing.

The state of the kitchen mortifies Remy, not pristine like she's used to, but dingy and lived in. She wipes off a space and cleans it thoroughly before pulling butter and eggs from the fridge. After, she searches through the dry storage and fridge (both are filthy and in need of a proper purge), gathering the spices, flour, and sugar she finds.

"I believe I have enough to whip up something that will melt in your mouth," Remy says to Amelia, smiling.

"Good, I doctored these bowls right. Maybe I can watch you bake?" Amelia asks.

"Get a little dirty together?" Remy responds with a wink, trying to hold on to the feeling that everything is fine, she's fine.

Amelia blushes and smiles. The phone rings, startling the women.

Amelia picks it up. "Ruby's, this is Amelia… Yeah she's up, Remy Kensington from West London… Shut up, Georgia," Amelia giggles and bats at the phone, its rather endearing. "Mama is with Auntie Tamika and Auntie Rose, we just saw the doctor yesterday, so she should be okay." She laughs and rolls her eyes. "You're the worst, whatever, same, love y'all be safe." Amelia hangs up the phone and turns to Remy. "Georgia wanted to check in on you. They tried to dig over, but couldn't even open the door."

Remy's face falls, she's going to end up in this shithole country for the holiday. "That doesn't bode well for me getting on a plane, does it?"

She follows Amelia as they walk back into the diner.

Amelia shakes her head. "I'm so sorry, I know you don't want to be stuck here for Christmas."

"Well, at least I'm stuck here with you," Remy responds with a small smile reaching out and putting a hand on Amelia's.

Amelia laughs so hard she nearly drops the chilli, she sets the bowls on the counter and leans against it. "Girl, has a line like that ever worked for you?"

Remy tries to run a hand through her hair. It's still damp and the melted snow has caused her hair relaxer to wash away and her short hair to curl up into its natural cloudlike curls. *Play it cool.* Remy grins. "I get away with quite a lot because…"

"Of your accent," Amelia finishes, taking a deep breath and wiping her eyes. "Thank you, I haven't laughed that hard in a long time."

"I have…"

"Plenty of ways you could make me laugh. Oh, I'm on to you Remy Kensington, I got your number."

"Not yet, but I can give it to you," Remy says with a wink and another mischievous smile.

Amelia gives Remy a side eye with a smirk. "Two can play at this game. I bet I could get you all sorts of buttered up if I laid on the southern charm.

Remy grins. "I say we both lay it on thick, win/win either way."

Amelia chuckles and shakes her head. "Let's eat first; you had us worried when Georgia came running in here with you." She sits at the counter, curling a leg up under her.

Remy sits next to Amelia and takes a small bite of the chilli. Most definitely a bowl full of things that are not on her diet, it tastes delightful but guilt gnaws at her. She's not supposed to stray from her diet, she can't go over eight and a half stone. "Yes, I'm not dressed for a trek through the snow. When I got stuck, I stupidly thought the whiskey would help keep me warm. I thought I read something about alcohol being good in the cold. Do we still have the bottle?"

Amelia nods. "I'm sure we do, and Ruby got permission to have a tap, she serves Schlitz, but you shouldn't be drinking alcohol right now, you need to let yourself heal."

Remy has no idea what Schlitz is and is afraid to ask. "Erm, well we have plenty of food, it's warm, this isn't an awful way to spend a night."

"Does the chilli pass your standards?" Amelia asks, bringing a heaping spoonful up to her lush lips.

Have another bite, Piggy.

Remy swallows another bite. The guilt has turned into the taunting voices of everyone that commented on her body and weight and everything else Remy worked so hard to get rid of. "Quite good, like my soul is warming."

Amelia's expressive face knits with concern. "Looks like it hurts to swallow. Are you okay?"

Remy shrugs, her throat feels like it's closing up. She may vomit, but that wouldn't be the worst thing.

Amelia reaches over and puts a warm hand over Remy's and gently squeezes it. "Ah, tell the little voice in your head to shut the hell up, Remy. One bowl of chilli won't derail whatever work you think you need to be doing."

Remy doesn't know how to respond, it's like Amelia is inside her head, listening to the battle being waged. "You mentioned a doctor, is your mum okay?"

Amelia shakes her head. "Ovarian cancer. She's been fighting it for the last year, but it looks like the cancer may be winning."

Amelia takes a bite of chilli, keeping her focus on the counter, clearly willing the tears to go away.

Remy reaches over and tentatively takes Amelia's hand, squeezing lightly. "I'm so sorry to hear that, Amelia. I'm sure she'll be all right."

Amelia gives a wan smile. "I can almost believe it when you say it."

"The accent," Remy responds with what she hopes is a reassuring smile.

"What about you? Are your parents in London, too?"

Remy nods. "Father sits on the House of Lords, mother runs a charity for children in Nigeria. My older sister, Elizabeth, plays cello in the London Philharmonic and has always done everything right my younger sister, Violet's a yummy mummy that can't do anything wrong. I used to be the fat girl they hid at picture times, now I have fully embraced my role as black sheep. Complete with splashing about the tabloids and getting arrested once a year for good measure."

"None of that is who you are though," Amelia says with

confidence.

Remy laughs. "Oh, is this where you psychoanalyse me?"

Amelia smiles over the rim of her coffee mug. "Well, I could? I have PhDs from Howard and Harvard, came home to take care of Mama."

"Oh, that makes you sexier, sorry, not sorry. Well, Doc, you've been holding out on me."

Amelia shrugs slyly and rolls her shoulders and neck. "Sometimes you look at someone and take a guess at what they're like. I wanted to make sure I hadn't lost my edge. Back home in Chicago I can walk into a club and tell you exactly who I will and won't consider going home with."

Remy's smile widens. "Alright clever clogs, so you're not like others I can charm with a bright smile and clever quip, then?"

Amelia chuckles. "Sorry, you'll have to work harder here."

I may still get you yet. "What's your favourite pastry? Something that instantly makes you happy?"

"Mama's Chess Pie, it's a staple 'round here," Amelia answers without missing a beat.

Remy cocks her head, a pastry she hasn't heard of. "I don't know what that is, but I'm sure I'll crack it. Do I get a recipe, or should I guess?"

"Have you ever watched the Great British Baking Showdown?" Amelia asks.

Oh aces, this is how I'll get you, doctor. Remy nods and runs a hand through her hair. "I was a contestant during the celebrity charity event, washed up child reality star turned pastry chef. Did that air over here?"

Amelia laughs. "Shut up, no you weren't!"

Remy nods and swallows another small bite of chilli, it immediately turns to a rock in her stomach. She needs to expel everything. "I won twenty-five thousand pounds for charity water."

"If I had my cellphone, you know I'd be googling that," Amelia says, finishing her coffee.

The tone Amelia's using is probably supposed to be playful but there's something about being called a liar that always causes Remy to bristle. She is a lot of things but she's not a liar. "I don't know if my handbag made it but my phone is in there and I have photographic evidence."

Amelia cocks her head slightly with an examining gaze. "Well, they do that thing, um, the blind bake?"

"That was my favourite part! I actually do something like that at my restaurant in Belgravia. People email me recipes from all over the world for special occasions." Remy loves the challenge of it, a brief competition. "Now I'm loving this even more. Give me a list of ingredients for chess pie and I'll see what I can do."

Remy can't force herself to eat anymore, but Amelia is done. So Remy takes the chilli bowls to the kitchen. Amelia eyes Remy's full bowl but thankfully says nothing, instead starting the list. The snow has piled up higher against both doors, and it's creeping up the windows.

Remy looks around the kitchen for her bottle of Jack and bag, but doesn't see either. She doesn't care if she should or shouldn't drink; she needs one. With a deep breath, she pushes into the diner and glances behind the counter then by the door. Snow has blown up against the doors and windows effectively burying them.

"How's that list coming?" Remy asks, rubbing her shoulders, she's sore and tired, she's not an ice lolly though. The fact she can't leave is settling in and her stomach is in her throat, the walls are closing in. Panic causing her skin to crawl.

Amelia looks up and smiles. "Almost got it. You okay?"

"No, where's the tap? My nerves are jangled, I'm not good at being stuck. It's worth the risk for me, I need a beer."

Amelia waffles, chewing her lip, but finally points to the other end of the diner. "Just at the end of the bar. I'll grab the beers, you can grab the list and start getting your ingredients."

Remy smiles. "Brilliant, are you going to set a timer for me?"

Amelia shakes her head. "I think the ingredients themselves are enough."

Remy laughs and grabs the list, taking it to the kitchen. Most of it is pretty benign and looks similar to a custard tart.

Remy starts by cleaning, incapable of baking in a messy kitchen. Dirty dishes go into the sink for a soak, wipe the prep tables down, and a quick sweep. As she's sweeping, she knocks the bottle of Jack Daniel's and it skitters across the floor. She stoops and grabs the bottle, looking where it was and sees her bag. When she sits up, Amelia's leaning against the door frame holding two pint glasses both half empty.

"Couldn't resist a quick peek?" Remy asks, grinning.

Amelia tuts and shakes her head. "Girl, I don't know what you're talking about. Found your purse?"

Remy nods and shuffles through it. Everything is still there, and her phone turns on. She takes a sip from the bottle and cringes. "This is truly awful."

Amelia takes the bottle from Remy and takes a sip. "It grows on you, as does this." She scoots Remy's pint to her.

"Bottoms up, or tops down, depending on how you want to look at it." Remy sips the vile lager, pulling a face at the pint.

Amelia chuckles. "Need help finding anything on the list?"

"Perhaps a few things off the list." Remy winks and Amelia rolls her eyes.

Remy opens her phone and clicks on her photos, she pulls up her album from the show. "Here, I'm a lot of things but I rarely lie."

Amelia's mouth drops. "Damn girl."

Remy floats around the kitchen, quickly pulling out the ingredients and tools she'll need. In minutes, the crust is in the oven for a par-bake. Cleaning and baking help shake the fog away and firmly plant herself in kitchen mode. She's fine, everything's fine.

Amelia erupts in deep belly laughs. "You have naked pictures of yourself on your phone?!"

Remy turns to Amelia. "I don't remember taking any naked photos…"

Amelia turns the phone to Remy who starts laughing hysterically. She has to put down the knife she's using.

"Oh, I forgot about that! A dare from Pierre, another contestant. He cut a check for a thousand quid to my charity for that."

"How much is that?" Amelia asks.

Remy chews on her lip and looks up to the right. "Oh, erm, I'm shite at math, sorry," she finally says with a shrug.

"Wonder what I could get you to do for a thousand quid?" Amelia tosses over the rim of her pint glass.

"You don't have to pay, I'm yours," Remy responds with a wink.

Amelia rolls her eyes. "You and your lines. How's that pie coming?"

"An artist never rushes their masterpiece." The lights flicker and Remy looks around the small space. "What's the backup plan if we lose power?"

"Get creative?" Amelia responds, shrugging.

Remy smiles; she's even better when she can do what she wants with the ingredients. "Deconstructed chess pie as a backup, perfect. So tell me something you would never tell another soul, give me one of your dirty little secrets."

"Only if you play, too," Amelia states.

"Happily, I am only going home because Vie is raising her

child genderless and I cannot wait to see my parents fall over themselves trying to appease her. She's an idiot, but for some reason they fawn all over her."

"Sensing a touch of hostility there," Amelia says in a voice that mimics Remy's therapist back home.

Remy's chest gets hot and her cheeks flush. Deep breaths push the anger back down. "Enough to stuff a cat with. If I was to come home with a genderless child, they'd rack me. She gets formal invites and the whole nine. I win six James Beard Awards and nearly land a Michelin star, they tell me I should get a proper job."

A quick flash of understanding and pity flashes across Amelia's expressive face. "My baby sister, Lane, gets away with murder, too. Not literally, but Mama and Daddy let her off with a warning, where I'd be grounded for life. I think it's something that just happens."

The lights flicker again. This time, they lose power for a few seconds before it comes back on.

4

Remy kicks into high gear expertly mixing and prepping without using a single measuring device. At one point, she shows off by getting the crust out while continuing to mix. Amelia just sips her beer and watches.

Remy gets the pie in the oven and sets a timer on her phone. "In about ten minutes, I'll drop the temp on that and let it continue to bake for forty minutes. How will we waste the time?"

"Beer and banter?" Amelia asks.

Remy nods. "Want to play a bit of never have I ever?"

"Never have I ever used my British accent to get in a lady's drawers," Amelia says with a disarming smirk. "Like that, right?"

Remy laughs. "What are drawers? Like a chest of drawers?"

"No drawers like undergarments," Amelia responds, laughing harder.

"Oh, you mean knickers?" Remy asks.

Amelia's forehead knits, and she cocks her head. "Knickers?"

Remy nods. "You know like uh… Panties?"

"Yeah, that's what I was saying." Amelia laughs. "Drawers

is another word for knickers, then. So I have never used my British accent to get in a lady's knickers."

Remy laughs and takes a drink. "Come now, surely you used your southern charm to seduce folks in Chicago."

Amelia shakes her head and shrugs. "Nah, I enjoy talking with a person and forming a bond; I was never good at hookin' up."

Remy puts her hand on her chest and bows slightly. "I'm happy to help you with that."

Amelia shakes her head with a chuckle. "Mm-hmm, I'm sure you would. Ain't gonna happen, slick."

Remy has yet to encounter someone this difficult to charm. Perhaps she got her wish and found someone that's going to call her on her bullshit and make this interesting. "Because?"

Amelia makes eye contact and holds it. "I refuse to be another successful conquest. You're all sorts of sexy and it's been way too long, but I'd hate myself if I gave in."

Remy isn't prepared to find her stomach back in her throat and tears welling up. She takes a drink of her beer so she can brush them away. "I'm not a wanker."

Amelia's immediately sorry, and it's written across her face and posture. She reaches out and puts a hand over Remy's. "Whoa, that was a pretty big reaction, I'm so sorry."

"I wasn't prepared for that either," Remy admits as the tears fall. She clears her throat, trying to get the emotions out of her voice. "Oh, you got me, Doc..." Remy's words fall away and she takes another sip of the whiskey.

Come now, cry for us, Piggy.

"I know you're a good person, just wounded." Amelia has a comforting tone to her voice, the walls she surrounded herself with drop.

Remy breaks, face in her hands, leaning forward to hide the tears. Amelia takes Remy in her arms and holds her, her hand runs along Remy's back, the warmth from the friction radiates up and down, following the motion of Amelia's hand.

Get a hold of yourself. First you're eating a bowl of fat, now you're crying like a child. She scolds herself silently.

Remy tries to take deep breaths to bury the pesky tears. "Sorry, this isn't very British of me, I'm making a bit of a scene." Remy takes another deep breath. "If I died today, I would have gone out a brash wanker that ran through women like most go through tissues."

"Mm-hmm, and how does that make you feel?" Amelia asks, back to that therapist's tone of hers.

Remy takes another deep breath and buries the emotions again. The severity of her earlier predicament finally settling. "I'm not a bad person, and wouldn't want you to hate yourself for sleeping with me. Honestly, I don't know how to *not* be a brash wanker, it's what women expect from me."

"Let your walls down and be who you want to be?" Amelia suggests, still holding Remy, comforting her.

The timer goes off and Remy doesn't want to stand up; she wants to stay wrapped up in Amelia's presence. She pushes to her feet and goes to readjust the temperature of the oven. "Being the Bad Girl of British Baking is easier than the dreadfully awkward woman that just wants to make people happy with her food," Remy admits, surprised by her honesty.

Amelia gives Remy a knowing smile and sips her beer. "Well, you can be painfully awkward with me. No judgement, and I promise not to let anyone know that you're a kind person."

Remy laughs. "Thank you for that. Sometimes I feel my reputation is all I have. If I move to LA, that's where I was before the diner, a new restaurant wants to bring me in as their Executive Pastry Chef. That's easier to get to, I can make you the dessert that nearly got us the Michelin star."

"That's a pretty big deal isn't it?" Amelia asks, her beer almost gone.

Remy nods. "We would have had it too, but the appetiser was off, and there was a spice issue with the main course. I was on point, the reviewer made it a point to tell me my skill is what he expects from restaurants trying for a star."

Amelia's clearly impressed, which makes the panic gripping Remy's chest loosen. "How did you get into baking?" she asks.

Remy doesn't want to think about the whys. "I hid in the kitchen growing up." The honest response surprising Remy again. Maybe Amelia will like her more if she's honest, though? "My parents' staff was kind and accepting. Our cook, Helga, was from Poland, she taught me everything she knew. When we were on holiday in the south of France, Francois, our chef there, taught me pastry. He told me I was a natural. I studied at Le Cordon Bleu and finished their pastry and wine programmes. Then started in the kitchens in France and Belgium before moving home to London with my sole focus on moving up to Executive Pastry Chef. There isn't time to eat and so many drugs, so I lost the weight and wasn't ridiculed anymore. Well, at least not for that."

Amelia puts a comforting hand on Remy's shoulder and squeezes lightly. "I understand, and I'm so sorry for my choice of words and the way they impacted you."

Remy laughs, pesky emotions safely locked away again, and finishes her beer. "Earlier, leaving the airport, I was thinking how nice it would be to find someone that called me out. I wasn't prepared for it to be here."

Amelia smiles and finishes her beer. "Well, I am happy to be that for you anytime, Kensington."

"I appreciate that, Doc."

Remy gives Amelia a quick peck on her cheek. As Remy is going to give her a kiss on her other cheek Amelia turns and their lips almost meet. She leans back and smiles at Remy. "We have a TV and VCR for when we used to do movie night Saturdays. How do you feel about making a flour sack fort and watching shitty movies?"

Remy nods. "Could be fun."

"Good. You mentioned weight a few times and bullies. Do I need to worry about you making yourself throw up?"

Damn, she's good. Remy had wondered how to find the loo discreetly. "Surely we can find other ways to work off the calories?" she says, trying to smirk. "I'm afraid the weight will come back and things will get bad again," she hears herself add. Shocked, she's talking about all these things she's supposed to just drink and fuck away.

"Want to talk about that fear and what things will get bad again means?" Amelia's horrible impression of Remy's accent is enough to keep her from panicking and being a right tit.

Remy is fairly certain if she tries she'll start crying again and she can't afford to make a bigger fool of herself. "I don't want to become a blubbering mess again…"

Amelia smiles, taking Remy's hand. "Well, I'm a safe place to turn into a blubbering mess. No one will ever know."

Remy takes a deep breath and shakes her head. "I can't talk about those things, drives my therapist mad."

"You can't, or don't want to?" Amelia asks.

Remi chuckles. The lights flicker. "Both?"

"Want to talk about why?"

Remy shrugs. "Well, the obvious, no one cares about me, so why should I bother?" she finishes the awful beer. "Then the pain it will cause for me—it hurts to remember the torment, so I'd rather not."

Pity party for Piggy.

"Surely there are people that care about you, Remy," Amelia states, her expressive face gathering pity and sympathy.

See that? No one cares. Now squeal for us, Piggy.

Remy shakes her head, fighting the urge to cry again. "If I had died today, no one would have mourned me, no one cares," she whispers, standing quickly and going to the tap. If she looks at Amelia, she'll start blubbering like a child again and she can't have that.

5

Amelia doesn't let Remy run. Instead, following her to the tap and refilling her own beer, expressive face mirroring the pain Remy tries so hard to bury. "Hey, you can't just say that and walk away, Kensington."

"If I'd stayed I would've started sobbing again," Remy admits, filling a second pint glass. "The gravity of my situation is finally settling in and I'm not sure how to deal with it, if I'm being honest."

Amelia smiles softly. "Something else we can talk about, should you want to. No one will know you cried, or let your guard down and were vulnerable."

"I will, I'm supposed to be better than this."

"What does that mean?" she asks, leaning against the counter sipping her beer.

Remy leans against the other counter. "I need to prove I'm not the same little fat girl crying in her wardrobe with biscuits reading cookbooks." She sips her beer. "Sometimes I hid in the pantry, but Helga would find me and she'd cook and food always helped. Which made everything worse because I was already so fat and ugly and needed to be losing weight not packing it on."

Have another bite, Piggy.

Amelia takes the beer from Remy's hands, sets it on the counter, and hugs her tightly. "None of the terrible things people said about you, or to you, are true. I'm so sorry so many people failed you and made you feel like a failure."

"With the accent, I can almost believe that," Remy says, hugging Amelia back.

Amelia chuckles, squeezing Remy before leaning back and making eye contact. "I'm serious, and I'm going to say it until you believe me."

Remy swipes at her eyes and takes a drink of the terrible beer, clearing her throat. "Perhaps by the end of our snowcation? But it's going to be hard to undo thirty-plus years of conditioning, no matter how fit the person saying it is."

"Well, at least now you know someone cares about you, Remy. We just met but I care what happens to you and want you to take care of yourself. I'm sure plenty of people do."

Go ahead and cry, you fucking disgrace.

Remy has a harder time forcing the tears down with the rest of her awful beer. "You must stop saying things like that, Doc."

"Hey, I'm just trying to get you to fall madly in love with me, so you'll decide to stay and I'll have someone interesting to talk to."

Remy laughs. "I've never loved nor been loved by anyone," she hears herself saying instead of making a smarmy comment. Hearing the truth out loud surprises her. "Sorry, I meant to take the piss. Let me try again."

Amelia is hugging her again. "You gotta stop breaking my heart here, Kensington."

"Well, if I do, you'll stop hugging me and I rather enjoy your hugs."

"I'm not gonna sleep with you but I'll hug you as much as you need." She makes eye contact, holding Remy's hands.

"You are worthy of love, you are lovable, you deserve to be loved."

The lights go out and stay out for a minute, giving Remy time to get her emotions in check.

Piggy and her unbecoming feelings. Blubbering away because no one will be her friend.

Remy can't run it out, they're stuck in this diner. She needs to find another way to release and regain control. She moves away from Amelia to find the loo, she'll purge until she's vomiting blood, that always helps.

Amelia steps in front of Remy.

"Let me go," Remy says halfheartedly, trying to move around Amelia.

Come now, Piggy, where are you running? Have another pudding.

"No, Remy, I won't do that," Amelia whispers, opening her arms.

As much as Remy wants to fight it, she lets Amelia stop her, melting into the hug instead. She doesn't register the words coming from her mouth, only the even reassurances from Amelia she's safe and loved and supported. But she isn't. How can she be? No one could love something like her. She's unlovable. A fat, unlovable cow, a worthless failure.

I wouldn't trust you running a bath, let alone a kitchen, you worthless bitch.

Amelia leans back, puts her hands on Remy's cheeks and kisses her. Wow, her lips are soft and she tastes like coffee and spices. Amelia leans back again, tears streaming down her cheeks.

"Sorry, I should have asked, but Remy Kensington you gotta stop breaking my heart. Repeat after me—"

"If spilling my secrets will earn another kiss, have them all," Remy murmurs.

Amelia smiles. "Repeat after me. I, Remy Kensington,"
Remy takes another choppy breath. "I, Remy Kensington,"
"Am worthy of love," Amelia says.

No one can love something as despicable as you.

Remy looks down. "Am I?"

Amelia looks like she may kiss Remy again, instead she gently rests her soft callused hands on Remy's angular jaw. "Repeat after me: I, Remy Kensington, am worthy of love."

The more she says it, the more Remy can almost believe it, almost. "I, Remy Kensington, am worthy of love?"

"Like you mean it," Amelia says softly, eyes still glistening with unshed tears.

Remy shakes her head and shrugs. The schoolyard taunts and decades of indifference echoing louder than her desire to believe the things Amelia is saying.

This isn't dessert, it's a fucking disaster, you untalented cunt.

Amelia gently pulls Remy down and leans in carefully resting her forehead on Remy's. "I know you have a lot of voices in that beautiful head of yours screaming horrible things at you. Do you have ways of getting them to quiet down?"

"I drink and fuck them away. When I can't do that, I throw up and run. None of which I can do right now; I was quite serious, I won't do anything without explicit and enthusiastic consent."

"Want to try something else?"

Remy shrugs, chewing her lip. "Kissing?"

Amelia chuckles and smirks. "Something even better."

Remy takes a deep breath. She can't say anything just nods slightly.

"Okay, so we can do this one of two ways. We'll see which one is best for you, okay?"

Remy takes a sip of beer and nods again.

"We're going to walk through a guided meditation together. Let's sit down, take my hands, and listen to my voice."

6

The longer Remy follows Amelia the easier it gets to shut down the inner voices that are always chiding her. The lights flicker again, casting the diner in inky darkness. Remy squeezes Amelia's hand a little tighter. Being stuck in the dark is never good for Remy, panic bubbles up, gripping her chest.

Come now, Piggy, time for your favourite game.

"Remy Kensington, there are no monsters in this dark. I'll scare them away, okay? Want to come—"

"I'll stay with you, thank you—" Remy says quickly with a deep breath.

"Want to talk about it?"

Remy shakes her head, then realises Amelia can't see her. "No, erm, no thank you, I'm not sure I can."

"If that changes, I'm here to listen, zero judgement."

Remy nods.

Amelia chuckles. "Did you nod? I can't see you."

Remy's turn to chuckle. "Yeah, yes I did… Thank you, that was helping. Sorry, I feel like I need to repay you somehow for everything you're doing for me."

Amelia squeezes Remy's hand and gives her a kiss on the cheek. "Good, I'm glad. You don't owe me anything, Remy,

I'm happy to help. Hold on to me, I used to work here, summers and after school. So I know my way around."

"So you grew up here?" Remy asks. Focusing on Amelia not the pins and needles and shadows that seem to breathe and whisper terrible things.

"Yeah, Georgia and I went to school together. Ruby gave me my first job outside Daddy's church. If we could get out of here, we're a five-minute bike ride to Mama's house. If you get stuck here, you'll come with me. Mama will put you to work in the kitchen, and my aunties will gush over your accent and ask you to say things. Sorry ahead of time."

"If I can't get home to watch the spectacle, I'll be happy to say anything your aunties want me to say and chop veg for your mama."

"They're all going to tell you you're too skinny. I'll tell them not to, I don't want to trigger you."

A torch clicks on and Remy smiles at the sincerity on Amelia's face. "Actually, it helps when people tell me I'm too skinny. Sometimes I'll look in the mirror and this grotesque monster is staring back. Then I get unhealthy in my habits."

Amelia's expressive face explodes with emotions. "Do we need to go into the bathroom and tell that monster staring back to fuck off? I can talk about the hella sexy woman you should see?"

"Perhaps? I'd rather enjoy watching you blush as you talked about all the ways I make you crumble."

Amelia laughs. "I am sorry I almost killed you, but I'm really glad you ended up here, Kenzie."

Remy laughs. "Kenzie?"

"I want to give you a good nickname, one that can override all the bad ones."

Thankfully, the timer goes off, giving her something other than the strange feelings bubbling up to focus on.

"It may need a little more time. Can you come check with

me?"

Amelia nods and they follow the torchlight into the kitchen, which is warmer than the lobby. She stops the timer and opens the oven. The pie looks done, Remy likes the colour and there's enough jiggle. She takes it out of the oven and starts back towards the lobby. "I'm going to put it by the windows to cool."

"Want to build the flour fort while we wait?" Amelia asks.

Remy nods. There is definitely a temperature difference, she goes over to the windows, a chill radiates off of them.

"With how cold it is over here, I'll check in twenty minutes, it may need longer."

"It smells like Mama's, I'd eat it hot, I don't care," Amelia says, smiling.

Remy shakes her head and tuts her tongue. "None of that! My food is too good to be shovelled in your face before its ready. Besides, I need to put the finishing touches on it."

Amelia chuckles. "I bet there's a joke in there about my pie in your face, Kenzie."

Remy laughs. "Look at you cracking sex jokes, Doc, I'm rubbing off on you."

"There will be no rubbing off on me tonight," she responds grinning, face flushed.

Remy laughs harder. "Oh, the blush you gave yourself."

"Talking like that here is like saying it in Mama's house or church."

They move back into the kitchen. Remy left the oven open so the heat has kicked things up to cosy. She follows Amelia to a storage space where a rather ancient television sits next to an even older generator.

"Wait, should we really use power to watch movies? Isn't it better to keep the generator for the fridge or freezer? We don't want Ruby to lose all her food," Remy says.

Amelia chews her lip and looks around. "What if we bring

snow in and pack the food? Or put the food outside? I'll follow your lead on this, I don't know what's going to be best."

"If the power stays off we'll decide then, okay?" Remy responds.

Amelia nods. "Dry storage is right here," she points, and Remy shudders.

"Bloody hell, this entire kitchen is such a mess, I may need to clean."

Amelia smiles. "If you'd rather clean than cuddle, I can help."

"Really?" Remy asks.

Amelia nods. "Yeah, I just want to spend time with you. Doesn't matter what we're doing."

Remy's flabbergasted. "Wait… You actually *want* to spend time with me?"

Amelia nods, cocking her head. "Yeah, I like you Kenzie, I'm having a good time, even if you keep breaking my heart."

"Oh, I may cry again if you say things like that Doc. People don't enjoy spending time with me unless they can get something from me. You'll actually clean someone else's kitchen with me, and you're not just saying that?"

Amelia kisses Remy's cheek. "Yeah, we have all night, we can watch movies and build a fort later."

Remy blinks back tears and takes a sip of her beer. "Thank you, I would honestly get a smack if I let my kitchen get this filthy—"

"Wait, someone would hit you if your kitchen wasn't up to their standards?" Amelia asks, interrupting.

Remy's surprised at Amelia's surprise. "Yes? But when you're cooking in the kitchens I've cooked in everything is to a higher standard. Plus, there are agencies that require a certain level of cleanliness."

Tears well up in Amelia's eyes, more feelings Remy can't

quite place etched on her face.

"Oh my god, I am so sorry someone hurt you like that," she whispers.

"Well, I deserved it—" Remy starts, trying to help.

"No!" Amelia says fiercely, interrupting. "Remy Kensington, no one can hit you."

Remy's brow furrows. "But—"

Amelia shakes her head, black curls bouncing. "No buts! No one can hit or scream at you for any reason. They shouldn't be mean to you, you deserve more."

You're not even good enough to flip burgers at fucking McDonald's. Get out of my face before I make an example of you.

No, Remy deserves everything she gets, she's a worthless failure.

Amelia's emotions affect her voice, "Kenzie, you deserve more. Please say you believe that."

Remy bites her lip gaze cast down, shaking her head slightly, positive she's going to sob if she tries.

Amelia hugs Remy, rubbing her back. "I am so sorry someone hurt you so deeply and so often you started to believe you deserve it."

Remy shrugs and fidgets unsure how to respond.

"Would it help if we stopped talking and started cleaning?"

Remy nods, still certain she'll start sobbing if she opens her mouth.

Amelia doesn't push Remy, just helps get the cleaning supplies out. Remy starts with cleaning and organising the dry storage, chucking the expired food. She's already feeling better.

"You're the first person to tell me I didn't, don't, deserve that," Remy whispers, finally sure she can get the words out without making a fool of herself.

"Kenzie, you deserve to have someone tell you how wonderful you are every day. I've only known you a couple hours and I can tell that clear as day. You are a pretty special person and you deserve good things."

Remy's throat closes up again and she's battling tears. She cleans, focusing on anything but the overwhelming emotions. Amelia doesn't say anything else just putters, cleaning with Remy.

7

The kitchen is clean, and Remy has a firm hold on her emotions. She turns to Amelia. "Thank you very much for the kind words you've had for me tonight, I genuinely appreciate it. Sorry for all the emotional labour you're doing on my behalf, I'll make it up to you somehow, promise."

"Something big happened and you need a safe space to process. If that means a little emotional labour on my part I'm fine with that, okay?" Amelia smiles. "Can we eat pie now, or do you need to clean more?"

Remy doesn't understand what Amelia's saying, then realises Amelia wants them both to eat pie. "Oh! No, I make desserts, I don't eat them."

"Really?" Amelia says surprised.

Remy nods. "Not on my diet. I used to love sweets, can't balloon up again."

Amelia sighs but instead of pushing says, "will you at least take a bite of my piece, please?"

Remy nods. "Because you've been so kind and I've never had Chess Pie. I want to know if I'm right about the flavour profile."

"I don't know if it helps or not? From an anatomical and medical standpoint, because of your near death experience you can eat thousands of extra calories and it won't turn to fat. Your body will burn it as fuel to help with healing and recovery. So the three bites of chilli earlier were gone before you swallowed. If you want, I can make you a salad. Is that what's on your approved diet?"

Remy nods. "Bare chicken, veg, and some grains."

"Okay, well, if Ruby has any cooked chicken we can pop that on your salad. I'll feel better if you eat something, anything."

Stop running, Piggy, you haven't finished your plate.

Panic bubbles up and Remy stumbles away. "Wait, no, I…"

"Oh, Kenzie, no, I'm sorry," Amelia takes Remy's hand. "Not a forced thing, an 'I care about you' thing, okay? People can want you to eat because they care about you. I care about you and want you to take care of yourself."

Remy bites her lip to keep from crying. "Why?"

Amelia doesn't flippantly throw out an answer; they walk to the front of the diner. It's bitter by the windows. "Because you're worth caring about. You're worthy of my time, energy, and kindness."

Remy shakes her head slightly. "No, I'm worthless…"

"Oh no, Kenzie," Amelia murmurs. "That's something some asshole told you. You are worthy of love, you are worthy of respect, you are worthy of being cared for."

Remy stuffs the feelings down, breathing them away. She touches the pie tin, it's cooled enough. Remy carries the pie back into the kitchen and puts it down. When she can't find a sieve, she uses one of her many hacks and gently dusts the pie with icing sugar and a little lemon zest. She cuts a piece for Amelia, slides it over to her with a fork, and takes a fork for herself.

Amelia takes a bite and moans. "Oh my god, Kenzie," she takes another bite, closing her eyes and savouring it. "This is incredible. I'm not calling you a liar, I'm just shocked this is your first time making chess pie. It's better than Mama's. I never met anyone that can outbake Mama."

Remy takes a small bite, she was right, it's like a custard tart. "It's really better than your mum's?"

Amelia nods still eating with her eyes closed. They pop open. "Oh, Mama! I need to call and check on her." She goes to the phone and takes it off the hook, dialling.

"Mama?"

"Oh, thank god. Where are you, honey?" Remy hears come out of the phone.

Amelia responds in a language Remy doesn't recognise before switching to English. "I'm safe at Ruby's with the most amazing woman. She's a chef from London, her name's Remy, and she just made a Chess Pie for the first time and you'd think she'd made a thousand."

"Hm, really?"

Amelia nods at the phone excitement colouring her words. "Mama, you gotta try her food! She's so good at this, I didn't even give her a recipe just a list of ingredients!"

"Well then, best bring this girl home with you, I need hands in the kitchen. Where's she at?"

Amelia gestures Remy over.

Remy cautiously approaches the phone, massaging her elbow. "Hello, Mrs Haskins, I promise not to get fresh with your daughter. She's a tremendous woman."

"Certainly is! Did she tell you that she graduated top of her class from Howard and Harvard?"

"No, she told me she'd let you and the aunties brag about her accomplishments. I would love to hear more, though; I suspect she's quite accomplished."

Mama pauses. "Well, why don't you come on home with Amelia for Christmas? I'll show off all her diplomas and fancy awards."

Oh, well, lots of pesky emotions want to bubble up with that offer. "I was supposed to go home, but I'm stuck here—unsure where here even is."

"Come be stuck with us, I can't wait to play in the kitchen with you, dear."

"Thank you, that means a lot, I look forward to it."

Remy realises she means it and genuinely wants to go home with Amelia.

"Now my sisters may want to do a bake off, see how this pie of yours stacks up. Think you're up for it?"

"Yes, Mrs Haskins, thank you," Remy keeps the tears from falling out.

"Oh, I wish I was there to give you a big mama hug. Amelia, dear, can you hug Remy for me?"

Amelia hugs Remy, and Remy is sobbing again. "Sorry, I shouldn't be making a scene."

Keep crying and see what happens, you talentless hack.

"Make a scene. God gives us tears for a reason, shed 'em well. I love you, be safe and stay—"

The line goes dead and Remy is trying and failing to get the tears to stop. Amelia lets her cry and comforts her in a way she's never been before.

Finally, Remy gets control of herself and stands in the middle of the diner breathing with Amelia.

"Come on," Amelia says, grabbing her piece of pie and settling in the pile of flour sacks and blankets Remy didn't even see her create. Remy settles with her. It has no right to be as comfortable as it is. Before Remy realises what's happening, she's curled up against Amelia, head resting on her chest.

"I should get up and take care of the food," Remy mumbles, listening to the slow even beating of Amelia's heart.

"Don't worry, it'll be fine, they share a wall with the outside. If the electricity doesn't kick back on itself, the generator will. Ruby's husband, Bubba, rigged it up, he's a genius with anything electrical."

Remy's eyes droop. "I'm tired…"

"Close your eyes, I got you."

Remy's never fallen asleep on someone before, but the weight of nearly dying and everything else drags her down into a fitful rest.

8

Nightmares come, like they do every night. Only this time, everything freezes and she's cracking and crumbling under shards of ice.

Panicking, Remy wakes up drenched in sweat, scampering away. Unsure if its memories, or nightmares, that have her trying to run. Knowing full well, there's never anywhere to run. When her back hits the wall, she brings her knees up to her chest and arms up to protect her face.

Soft, callused hands cautiously take hers and after a moment Remy realises its Amelia in front of her, not former classmates. She's in Ruby's dingy kitchen, she was asleep in their flour fort. The residual heat from baking is gone, the chill from outside finally seeping in and slowly sucking the heat from the air.

"Remzie," Amelia laughs at herself. Concern and support written across her beautiful, expressive face. "Sorry, Remy Kensington, do you remember me? Amelia Haskins. You had an accident, we're stuck in Ruby's Diner."

Remy doesn't know if she wants to laugh or cry, she can't shake the nightmares. "Nightmares, sorry," she murmurs, trying to take a deep breath.

"Want to talk about them?" Amelia asks, holding Remy's

hands rubbing her wrists.

Remy shrugs, rubbing her face, running her hands through her hair.

Amelia nods and gathers Remy up in her arms. "Want to lie back down together, or do you need to move around?"

Remy melts into the comfort of Amelia, gripping her tightly.

Amelia adjusts her pressure around Remy to match. "You're safe, you're cared for, you're protected," she murmurs.

"You must stop saying things like that. An award-winning pastry chef can't be stuck in… What state are we in? I don't even know where I am."

"We're near the border between Missouri and Oklahoma, practically straddling it. Some folks say this is Oklahoma, others Missouri. Occasionally we even get Arkansas. If Doctor Amelia Haskins PhD, can be stuck here, so can you."

"Wow, so you're a doctor-doctor, not just a PhD doctor?"

Amelia nods. "I'll let Mama brag about all the letters after my name, I hate doing that."

Surprisingly, Remi's phone rings. She was sure there was no signal, it's from her father.

"Hello?" Remy says.

Father's slightly laboured breathing punctures the static on the other end, as if he just ran to the phone. He clears his throat. "Driver is at Heathrow to collect you. Where are you?"

"Apparently on the border of Oklahoma and Missouri? Snow shut everything down, our plane diverted. I tried to drive to another airport but got stuck. So, I'm stranded in a diner, I almost died, it's been harrowing."

He huffs, clearing his throat. "Really, Rebecca Marie St. Clair Kensington, making stories again?" a disapproving cluck of his tongue pops loudly in her ear. "Very well, I will tell Liam he needn't wait. You owe him an apology, he battled London traffic for you."

"I almost died, I'm strand—" Remy repeats.

Father interrupts with an angry grumble. "Stop with the bloody—" the call drops.

"I'm sorry, Remzie…"

Remy chuckle sobs. "Is Remzie my new nickname?"

Amelia hugs her. "No, I just started with Remy and switched to Kenzie. Making stories again?"

Remy shakes her head, she can spill her secrets to this beautiful stranger but only if she can force the words out. Those words won't un-stick for anyone.

"Okay, if that changes—"

Remy knows it's rude to interrupt, but she does so anyway. "You're safe, I can spill my secrets and no one will be the wiser."

"Exactly. How can I best support you right now?"

"Surely you're tiring of me being so needy and troublesome. Just chuck me back in the snow."

Amelia rolls her eyes. "Nope, you're stuck with me. You're not being needy, something traumatic happened and you're processing."

"What time is it? Did you sleep?"

Amelia nods with a small smile. "We kind of slept on top of each other. I did what I could to protect the perishable food last night."

Remy squints at the clock. "Is it one am or pm?"

Amelia shrugs. "Want to go look out front?"

Remy wants to stay in Amelia's arms and let the panic and feelings melt away. She nods instead and stands, helping Amelia up. "I may need to do that breathing exercise if conditions are much worse…"

"We'll find a fun way to pass the time, or we'll dig out and walk to Mama's, okay?"

Remy nods. "Thank you. Being still leads to all the voices getting louder."

"If you want, we can do the exercises to quiet them?"

"Yes, I think I would."

Sunlight diffuses through the storm grey sky, snow still falls in heavy sheets.

"Oh nice, we slept half the day away," Amelia offers.

Remy can't say anything smart about lying around panic is strangling her. Snow drifts cover the front doors. Remy moves quickly back through the kitchen and swings the rear kitchen door open. It's a wall of snow that's packed into shelves, most the perishables are on them. The panic dies a little, Remy laughs. "Did you do this?"

Amelia bites her full bottom lip with a slight shrug and nod. "The freezer was so cold I couldn't walk in, but the cooler wasn't as cold… Will this work?"

Remy nods, shaking her hands. Pins and needles are marching up and down her arms, vision tunnelling, breath coming in quick gasps.

"Remzie, you're having a panic attack. Let's take deep breaths and try to calm down, okay?"

It's not okay, Remy's stuck, she can't run, she can't move, she's in this horrid country, with a not so horrid person.

"Okay, Remy, let's try to take some slow deep breaths, you need to slow your breathing down."

Amelia gently shuts the door and takes Remy's hands, rubbing her wrists and counting.

"Breathe in for five, breathe out for five, I'll count, just breathe."

As Remy listens to Amelia and lets her guide the thing, breathing gets easier and the pins and needles dissipate.

"There you go. Let's do a few more, then we can try to get the range working and cook."

Remy shakes her hands out and rolls her shoulders. "Yes, if I'm stuck at least I can cook for you, it's a small way to repay you for everything you're doing for me."

"Only if you make something you'll eat, too. Deal?"

Remy rolls her eyes. "Okay," she sighs.

"Anything, eggs and toast, or fruit and yoghurt? You just need more than three bites of chilli and a bite of pie, please?"

Remy studies Amelia. The concern causes her forehead to crease and mouth to twist in a rather cute pout, other emotions Remy can't identify mingling with the worry. There is no way to tell this face no, she nods instead. "Any allergies?"

Amelia shakes her head. "Do you?"

Remy takes another deep breath. "I doubt there's any rose water or lavender oil, so I'll be fine."

"There may be lavender in the ladies' room soap?"

Remy chuckles. "Probably not the kind I have issues with. Though I need to make use of the facilities, where is the loo?"

Amelia takes Remy's hand. "I'll show you, I need to go too." Amelia chuckles. "There are two singles, so we don't have to share a bathroom."

Remy blushes and looks down. "I'll have sex in public toilets, but I can't use them with anyone else. I had some rather nasty experiences at Luckley, so I avoid them."

Amelia pulls Remy into a gentle hug. "I'm sorry you experienced that. Is that another thing you need to talk about but can't?"

Remy nods. "My therapist keeps telling me I need to actually talk to her and work through the trauma or else I'm just paying to chat with someone."

Amelia nods. "I know the work is hard, but it helps. Do you want to take the flashlight? There are windows, so I'll be fine."

Remy takes the torch. "Thank you."

Amelia nods and turns into the men's, Remy turns into the women's. Snow piles up outside the window. Remy can't let herself panic.

9

When she's done, Remy forces the window open to determine if she and Amelia might get out of the diner. She doesn't care where they go, but Remy needs the option to leave.

"Remy?" Amelia says from outside the door.

"Yes, come in!" Remy calls.

Amelia pokes her head in and laughs. "What are you doing?"

Remy glances back over her shoulder. "You said your mum is close, we can walk there?"

Amelia smiles softly. "I'm not sure we could make it. But we can certainly try to get to Ruby's? From there, we can gear up and trek to Mama's, or stay here. Don't worry, you're not stuck. No one will keep you here. Let's go make something to eat. Would cooking help?"

Remy nods and stops trying to climb out the window. "Okay, yes. I can make you my favourite breakfast?"

Amelia nods. "If it's even a quarter as good as that Chess Pie I'm sure I'll love it. You're going to eat too, right?"

Remy runs a hand through her curls, fidgeting with one in the back. "If the voices get too loud, we can do that thing again, it helped."

Amelia smiles warmly. "Good, I'm glad."

They go back into the kitchen and Remy checks the range, she's grateful to see its gas. "We're in luck this is a gas range, so long as the gas service doesn't shut off we can cook. We can also use it for heat, but there are better ways to stay warm."

Amelia laughs. "I love your sense of humour, Kenzie."

"Who says I'm joking?" Remy asks with a wink and smirk.

Amelia laughs harder casually putting an arm around Remy's shoulders. "Oh, I am so fucking happy I met you. We're going to be friends for a lifetime, accept it."

"Maybe even more than friends? With all this snow, I suspect I have time to make you fall madly in love with me."

Amelia grins, eyes sparkling. "There's the confident brit I'm falling for."

Remy chuckles. "Let's check your snow fridge and our options."

She opens the snow fridge and finds some eggs and veg that's not too bad off. The state of the cast iron horrifies Remy. Everything in this kitchen needs tended to. Shining the torch on the flattop, she cringes. "I'm afraid before we can eat I need to clean. No one should eat anything off this."

"Want my help?" Amelia asks.

Remy feels that same gentle punch in the gut that this relative stranger is happy to clean with her.

Amelia's face falls. "Sorry, are you okay? Did I say something wrong?"

Remy shakes her head. "Quite the opposite," she clears her throat. "I'll be pouring more feelings out if I'm not careful."

Amelia flashes Remy her soft smile and runs a hand through her curls. "Do you want help?"

Remy nods. "If you don't mind? We need to give this a proper scrub."

"Absolutely, I don't care what we do, I just enjoy your company."

Remy bites her lip, fidgeting with the sleeve of the oversized tracksuit. "I'm not sure what to do when you say things like that."

This isn't good, Remy can't find the proper cleaner.

"They don't appear to own the necessary cleaner, which means I'm not sure it's been cleaned. That's rather frightening. How often do you eat here?"

"With a cook like Mama? Rarely. Is this actually bad or bad because of the trauma we're ignoring?" Amelia asks, casually leaning against the prep table.

"A bit of both, I imagine, if I'm honest."

Remy mixes up something that will suffice since she can't find the proper cleaner, then takes a scouring pad and scrubs. Amelia cleans next to her for a bit before turning. "Want to do a rapid fire first date questions?"

"I don't date much," Remy admits. "And when I'm bringing someone home from the club or pub we're not talking."

Amelia is taken aback, she shakes her head. "I'm genuinely shocked you're not constantly dating."

"I'm fit, but I work ninety hours a week. Then I go to the gym six days a week. And I sleep six hours a night when I'm lucky. So I haven't time for dating."

"When was your last proper date?"

Remy bites her lip and looks up and to the right, trying to remember. "Hm, the occasional event with Kona, an acquaintance back home, I'm not sure those count? The fling in LA was just sex. I believe the last proper date was with Shelly two years ago. Roughly three months in she realised what a worthless disaster I am and left."

Amelia tuts her tongue and shakes her head. "Her loss, you're a wonderful person, Remy."

"No, you're ignoring how awful I am because you almost killed me."

"Not true, you're not awful," Amelia responds.

Pity party for Piggy.

"Tell the little voice to fuck off, Remzie, you're not awful and it's okay to admit that."

Remy nods and musters up a smile. "I can almost believe that when you say it."

"The accent," she says with a wink. "Am I doing this right? I was a server, I got folk food, we're not allowed back here."

Remy chuckles. "Understandable, servers can't get near our kitchens either. If the servers want something, they ask Marco, or the expediters, and they relay it to us."

"What happens if a server comes into your kitchen?"

Remy can't let herself think about that, she shakes her head with a deep breath. "It's only happened once, no one has made that mistake since."

Amelia's expressive face explodes with sympathy but she doesn't press which Remy is grateful for.

"Does your current kitchen contribute to the trauma and nightmares, or is it better?"

Remy's not sure how to answer that, she shrugs. "We have a lot of pressure on us, we're trying for a star."

"That's a great non-answer."

Remy fidgets, focusing on a spot and scrubbing. Amelia doesn't push it, she just goes back to scrubbing, too.

10

The filth covering the flat top slowly dissolves away with the magic cleaning solution Remy threw together. It's almost clean enough to use again, silver no longer black.

"I want a kitchen where I can make things better," Remy finally says.

"Is that why you're considering moving thousands of miles to L.A.?"

Remy shrugs. "I'd rather not move to this shithole country. No offence."

Amelia shoots Remy an understanding smile. "I'm a Black woman in the South, I completely understand."

"Yes, I suppose you do. In L.A., blonde white women kept trying to touch my hair and asking what I am, it was rather insulting. Finally, I went and had my hair straightened, which helped some…" She focuses on a spot, finding the action of scrubbing it away relaxing. "I just—I'd have the control I want, and they're paying me nearly double what I make now. They want to do a TV pilot, and the Bad Girl of British Baking can help them land a spot."

"How would that make you feel? For people to assume you're the bad girl we both recognise you aren't?"

Remy shrugs, focusing on another spot. "Before the plane

diverted, I was ready to let a camera follow me into the restaurant in London, slap the wanker in charge, upturn a table, and storm out. Now?" Remy stops, emotions still bubbling below the surface when she thinks of what almost happened yesterday—she sighs. "I'm not sure what I want anymore."

"There's time to figure that out."

Remy nods, gets a clean towel and clean water, then does a final wipe down of the flat top and grease traps.

"Okay, now I can make us something delicious."

"I think I'm gonna have more pie too, I was dreaming about that pie."

Remy grins. "I'm glad you like it."

"Loved it, I love it, Remy, I'd eat it every day if I could. Honestly, you are so talented. Like you can hear someone is good, but it's another to experience it."

"The dreadfully awkward woman that wants to make people happy with her food is bursting," Remy admits. "Instead of doing a proper frittata, is a scramble alright?"

Amelia nods. "I just enjoy watching you cook." She blushes and winks, trying to give her own confident smirk.

"I'm quite fetching aren't I?" Remy responds.

Amelia blushes deeper.

Remy chuckles. "Want to help, or to get coffee or hot water for tea? Do you have breakfast tea?"

"Let me check for you."

Amelia leaves the torch and walks out into the front of the diner. Remy likes the quiet of the kitchen when it's like this. The dark is tolerable with the door to the front propped open, letting diffused light in.

"Remy, I have bad news, the coffee pot and tea kettle both need electricity, which we don't have," Amelia calls from the front.

"No bother, I'll whip something up if there's a kettle or pot."

"Judging by the way you were eyeing those pots and pans you don't want to use them."

Remy shakes her head. "No, they're not clean enough to make anything for human consumption."

Amelia chuckles. "They're clean just well loved, promise."

"There's a difference between being used and being filthy, but I'll clean more." Remy hopes that doesn't sound snippy, she can't believe the state of this kitchen.

Amelia doesn't seem bothered by the statement. "Okay, while we clean, what's your favourite colour?"

"Marigolds in the garden. Yours?" Remy responds. That was always one thing about the estate she loved is Viktor's landscaping. Viktor is Helga's husband and the groundskeeper, and he let Remy help care for the marigolds.

"Deep vibrant purple. Where'd you grow up?"

"The family estate, in Berkshire outside Reading. What was it like growing up here?"

Amelia does a stop, rewind hand gesture that is endearing. "Wait, a family estate? That sounds fancy. Do you hobnob with royalty?"

Remy shrugs, finding both talking with Amelia and the act of cleaning soothing. "If it's all the same, tell me about your family and growing up here. I have complicated feelings about mine, yours is much worthier of our time."

Amelia nods. "It's exactly what you'd expect it to be. There's only a thousand people in our town, you either stay and work your family farm or get out."

"From the sounds of it, you left, are incredibly successful, and gave up everything to care for your mum, yeah?"

Amelia shrugs with a shy smile. "I'll let Mama and the aunties brag. That's something I struggle with."

Remy finds that fascinating, someone as supportive and

outgoing as her should want to boast about their accomplishments. "Tell me to be proud, but downplay your accomplishments?"

Amelia laughs. "Something like that."

"What language were you two speaking on the phone? I didn't recognise it."

"A creole passed down through the family. Started when we were slaves and stuck around after we weren't anymore."

Remy nods slightly. Now everything is clean she can make tea or coffee.

"All of my best memories are from the kitchen with Helga or Francois, or the garden with Viktor. They're much kinder than my family—I guess, they were the love to a certain extent, it wasn't perfect or enough but it was something?"

"Are kitchens still a source of comfort, or are they part of the problem?" Amelia asks.

"Both? There isn't much I can do, but I try to make things in my little corner of the kitchen better?"

"So you agree being chastised, hit, and screamed at isn't okay?"

Remy nods. "But it doesn't mean that erases the voice telling me I'm different and deserve it."

Amelia's expressive face breaks. "Maybe I can help you erase that little voice."

Remy shrugs. "Perhaps? It's always been there, reinforcing the terrible things said and done by others."

"Well, it can fuck off, I'm here now," Amelia says with a warm smile. "What are you doing? That smells amazing."

Remy was on autopilot just doing, she has entire shifts she doesn't remember. "Oh! I hadn't realised I started a pot. Just a spiced drink I make when I don't have breakfast tea. Want coffee too?"

Amelia shakes her head breathing in through her nose with her eyes closed and a small smile playing on her kissable lips. "No, it's okay, I want to start with this, it's smells like Mama's house."

"Yeah?"

Amelia nods. "And I also want whatever's in the skillet, it smells amazing."

Remy didn't realise she'd been doing that either. She tips the food from the skillet onto two plates and pours the tea into mugs.

"You seemed surprised you had the stove going," Amelia says cautiously.

"Sorry, I don't remember starting any of it, I was on autopilot. Hopefully this tastes good?" Remy responds, wiping down the area she'd just been using.

"Do you go on autopilot often?" Amelia asks in her therapist voice. Remy wonders if she even registers she's doing that, or if her cadence just naturally shifts.

She nods, chewing her lip. "Sometimes it's as if I blink and I've lost days." Remy shrugs, massaging her elbow. "Probably not a good thing, but started happening—well, I guess it's something that's always happened, it seems to get worse as I get older."

"If you ever want to talk about it, or resources to ground yourself that's something we can do," Amelia says, taking a bite of breakfast. "Holy shit, Remy, this is amazing! Food never tastes this good here."

Remy appreciates the reminder Amelia can help without her pushing to help. Kona always tries to fix things without the slightest idea what Remy needs. Off Amelia's look, she takes a small bite and nods. "You'll have to let me make it for you again with proper ingredients. This isn't awful for how much improvising I did."

Amelia takes another bite and closes her eyes chewing slowly. "No making this better, it's perfect. The way you layer flavours is incredible. What's the biggest difference between this and how you usually make it?"

"Fresh herbs and veg, always use fresh when possible. I have a garden box at home I keep for when I have time to cook. The restaurant gets everything from the farm every morning."

"If you go to L.A. would you still do that?"

"Yes, hopefully, I only work with fresh ingredients—I'm making an exception here. Weather and all."

"Would your restaurant close if we were back home with weather like this?"

Remy takes another small bite, forcing herself to eat. This is on her diet, she can eat with no repercussions. "Oh, this sort of snow doesn't happen back home; I have to imagine we'd shut things down? Typically, we're open every day."

"Please don't tell me you work every day."

Remy shakes her head. "No, well, sometimes? I have in the past."

"What's the longest you've gone without a day off?" Amelia asks savouring another bite.

"Oh, I'd have probably offed myself had I kept track of those things. Two or three years? This snowcation is the first time I've had two days off in a row since I started working in kitchens."

Concern knits Amelia's brow in an endearing way and reaches over gently squeezing Remy's hand. "Will you get more time off if you move?"

Remy shakes her head. "No, if anything I'll be working more while we establish the restaurant. It's a hard thing to open and maintain."

"Would it be helpful to make a pros and cons list?" Amelia takes a sip of her tea. "This is amazing too! Can I talk you into staying in this tiny ass town and cooking for me? I'll pay you in hugs."

Remy laughs. "Don't tempt me, I quite like your hugs." She sips the tea. "This is also better with fresh ingredients, but it's not terrible."

Amelia takes Remy's hands in hers. "Remzie, you are fucking good at this. First the Chess Pie, then breakfast and tea? The flavours explode and it just makes me… Your food is like taking a bite of love. The fact you manage these flavours here is just incredible."

Remy takes another bite to swallow the feelings. "Thanks, Doc."

"Thank you for eating. Is this on your diet? Because we can eat it for every meal during our snowcation."

"And deny you the other wondrous things I do in the kitchen?"

"Oh, you have more tricks up your sleeve?" Amelia asks.

Remy tries to flash a disarming smirk. "Remember, I'm going to cook my way to your heart."

Amelia puts a hand to her chest. "You're already there," she smiles warmly. "Complete with my respect and admiration, too. You are the most talented person I've ever met."

Remy blinks back tears. "Really?"

"Yes! Without a doubt, I've never met anyone with half your talent, even. You can out cook everyone I know, even Mama, and Mama can make commodity cheese macaroni and hotdogs taste good." Amelia chuckles and takes another bite with a content sigh.

"I'm not sure what that is but I look forward to trying your mama's food."

"We'll get out and over there soon, I'm sure. I'm going to get pie. Do you want pie?"

Remy shakes her head. "I'll have a bite of yours though, I am rather hungry."

Amelia smiles. "If you want to try Ruby's chilli again I saved the leftovers?"

Remy runs a hand through her hair and shakes her head.

"No, I can't deviate that far from my diet without consequences. I don't miss days at the gym like this or just sit about."

"Well, we can run around the diner or dig out or something?" Amelia offers.

"With consent, there are wonderful ways to burn calories."

Amelia chuckles. "It has been too long, but I can't consent, it would be unethical. You're not okay, and I know you're not okay, so I can't be sure your consent is consent, if that makes sense."

Remy doesn't know how to feel about that, which annoyingly appears to be her new baseline. "Erm, I can pretend to be okay? Fear not, I'm totally fine now, nothing's wrong, nor has been wrong."

Amelia takes Remy's hand with that smile of hers that causes Remy's stomach to flip-flop. "Still a no. Want to cuddle and talk instead?"

If anyone had ever suggested something so ludicrous to Remy before she would have been a real wanker, but it doesn't sound awful when Amelia suggests it. "Oh, I've never done that before."

"Really? You've never sat on the couch and just enjoyed each other's company?" Amelia asks.

Remy shakes her head with a weak smile and half-hearted shrug.

Amelia leans over and tenderly kisses Remy's cheek, hugging her. "Well, if you want we can cuddle in the flour fort and talk?"

"Let me clean up the mess I made, then you can show me what you're talking about."

Amelia smirks. "Need help cleaning?"

Remy shakes her head. "Just give me a moment. Do you need more?"

Amelia shakes her head and takes a bite of pie with a content sigh. "I'll finish my pie and watch you clean. This is even better the next day. How do you get your flavours so rich and layered? Is there a secret?"

Remy is proud of how she layers flavours and the time she's put into learning all the best ways to make them pop. "Plenty of secrets, I'll spill them while we snog in the flour fort."

"Snog?"

"Or sorry, make out."

Amelia giggles blushing and does a cute shrug nod that makes Remy want to melt a little but she doesn't understand why.

"Do I need to tell the little voice to fuck off?"

Remy shakes her head with a smile. "No, no, I'm just… not sure what to do with everything I'm feeling…" she admits softly.

Amelia squeezes her hand. "Want to talk about what you're feeling?"

She shrugs. "If I can be honest? I'm not sure…"

Have a cry, Piggy, no one cares.

Remy shouldn't let her guard down; she's going to be hurt, and it's going to be her fault.

Stupid little girl, desperate for attention.

She turns so she can go make herself throw up and regain control, then she'll run until she passes out.

Amelia steps in front of her and takes Remy's hands in hers. "Hey, Kenzie, there's nothing wrong with anything you're feeling, or admitting you don't know what you're feeling. We can talk, or not talk, we can clean, or snog in the flour fort. Whatever you want to do."

Remy should push Amelia away, hurt her before she's

hurt.

Come on, you're a basketcase, this was inevitable.

Remy scoffs and pulls away from Amelia going towards the sink. She's a selfish, worthless nothing. No one cares about her, or wants her, certainly not someone as put together as Amelia. All of this is a mistake, she needs to stop it now.

"Remzie, you can't push me away, but you can't be a dick either. Come on, let's get the little voice to fuck off," Amelia says, taking Remy's hand.

Remy shakes her head. "Piss off, I don't want your help!"

No one cares enough to do anything.

"I'm not letting you push me away. Come on, I'm going to hug you while you fall to pieces, okay?" She gently takes Remy into her arms and hugs her close.

Remy wants to fight the comfort she doesn't deserve, the strange emotions swirling around, all of it.

Worthless bit.

"You deserve this."

Squeal for us, Piggy, you're about to get what you deserve.

The more Remy wants to pull away and get Amelia to fuck off, the harder Amelia hugs her and reassures her she's safe and everything will be okay.

Pity party, Piggy, no one will be her friend.

"Stop, I don't deserve this, I don't—" Remy falls to pieces, melting into the comfort and safety Amelia provides even though she doesn't deserve it.

"Shhh, you deserve this, Remy Kensington, you deserve to be happy and supported and cared for. You deserve to be told how special and important you are. I'm not going anywhere."

Remy can't stay standing, she crumples into Amelia fisting her shirt allowing the tears to leave her in heaving waves.

"Keep crying and see what happens!" Chef screams, throwing the plate at Remy.

"Fuck off, little voice. Remy can have feelings and express them. She's an amazing person and I enjoy spending time with her."

Somehow that has Remy crying harder, she curls into Amelia, soaking in the safety and comfort even if part of her still resists both.

It takes time to compose herself and stop sobbing so hard. She's curled into Amelia, sitting in her lap, head resting on her chest.

"Sorry, I shouldn't—"

"Be mean to yourself; we all have days we need to fall apart. Last week after Mama's doctor appointment was mine. Georgia pulled me over because I was swerving and I fell to pieces right there on the side of the highway."

"So you two are actual friends?"

Amelia nods, playing with Remy's hair in a comforting way. "Georgia isn't for everyone, but we've been friends since grade school."

Remy's eyes droop. "Why am I so tired?" she mumbles.

"Science," Amelia responds simply. "Want me to explain

it?"

Remy's going to say something snarky, but she can't seem to stay awake.

11

Nightmares have Remy scrambling when she wakes up. As with the last time she woke up in Ruby's, it takes a moment to realise it's Amelia there, she's safe. She's not where she had been, those things aren't happening.

"Kenzie, you here?" Amelia asks, rubbing her wrists.

Remy nods, taking a deep breath, or at least trying to. The pins and needles are in full effect and she can't seem to breathe.

"You're having another panic attack. Let's breathe together, you're here, you're safe."

Like last time, everything Amelia does helps, and Remy gets control of herself.

There's a wet spot on Amelia's chest and Remy may chuck herself back in the snow. "Don't tell me I was drooling on you?"

Amelia smiles sadly and bites her lip. "Mostly tears, you were crying and talking in your sleep." She gently squeezes Remy's hand. "I'm so sorry so many people failed you and those things happened."

Remy doesn't know how to respond, she runs a hand through her hair, damp from sweat. "How's the snow? Think we can dig out to Ruby's and get to your mama's house?"

Amelia nods. "If that's what you want to do, I'm happy to try. If it's too late to do it today, we can tomorrow, okay?"

Remy takes a deep breath, pushing it out, and shaking her hands. "Being stuck with you is nice, but we're still stuck which is not as nice."

Amelia gives Remy a grounding hug. "Yeah, it's been nice being stuck with you, too. Have I told you how glad I am we met and I got to eat your food?"

Remy blushes and wants to be a snarky asshole instead she lets the dreadfully awkward woman that just wants to make people happy with her food respond. "Thanks, Doc, I'm glad I met you too. I look forward to cooking with your mama and aunties. Will you be in the kitchen too?"

She chuckles and shakes her head. "No, I'm not allowed in Mama's kitchen, I nearly burnt it down last time I tried to cook."

"Really, how?"

Amelia blushes and glances down, fidgeting slightly. "Uh, I was boiling water and somehow almost caught the kitchen on fire?"

Remy can't help but laugh. "How? I'm not laughing at you, well, I'm trying not to laugh at you, I just can't... how?"

Amelia chuckles, blushing deeper. "Apparently I didn't put water in the pan—just the rice and spices?"

Remy can't help but lean in. "Sorry, may I kiss you?"

Amelia nods. There's no passion or heat, just the comfort of kissing Amelia. Remy rather enjoys kissing Amelia and wants to do more with her someday. "How much therapy do I need before you'll sleep with me? I enjoy kissing but I want to do more than kiss you."

Amelia smirks. "There isn't a metre, Remzie, you need to be okay, you're not okay."

"And I'm starting to be okay admitting that. Which my

therapist would say is a breakthrough, so progress?"

Amelia nods. "Progress. Want to see if there's enough daylight to dig to Ruby's?"

As much as she doesn't want to leave Amelia's comforting embrace the idea of getting a step closer to leaving helps stave off the panic roiling under the surface. Remy stands and helps Amelia to her feet.

Amelia laces her fingers through Remy's and shifts her arm so it's around her shoulders again. "Don't make fun of me, but I got used to your weight against me."

"Typically I would, to push you away, but I don't want to and that terrifies me…"

"Don't worry, I see you, Remzie, you can't push me away."

"This isn't a mistake, right? You're not trying to get me to drop my guard only to—"

Amelia stops Remy with a kiss. "Stop breaking my heart, Kensington."

"Then you may stop kissing me?"

Amelia chuckles. "Promise I'm not an asshole, I want nothing outside supporting you. Well, and possibly for you to cook more? Your food is seriously amazing."

Remy blushes and blinks back tears. "Honestly, I'm still surprised you want to spend time around me. I'm not sure how to handle it."

Before Remy can panic because the front of the store is dark, the phone rings, startling both of them.

"Ruby's Diner, this is Amelia."

"Heya, Lia, how's everything goin' over there?" Georgia's heavily accented voice booms out of the phone.

"Remy and I are doing okay, we want to make our way over there to gear up and hike to Mama's."

"In the morning, we'll start digging from the house. If you want to dig from the diner, we'll meet in the middle?" There's static, the call almost drops. "How's Mama? Were

you able to reach her?"
Amelia twirls the phone cord around her finger.
"Yesterday, she's fine."

"How's our beautiful Brit, you two shagged yet? I looked it up, that's what they call hookin' up," Georgia asks, a teasing quality to her voice.

Amelia blushes giggling. "Shut up, Georgia, no, no, we've kissed though, she's a fantastic kisser. Her chess pie is better than Mama's, though I'd never tell Mama that, and she made breakfast earlier that almost made me cry."

"Save some of that food for us. Maybe we can whip something up for lunch before helping you over to Mama's house? Be safe, stay warm."

"You too love you all!"

"Love you too, bye Lia."

Georgia hangs up, so does Amelia.

Remy smirks. "You're pretty cute when you giggle. If you need a story for your friends, you can say we shagged."

Amelia shakes her head. "No, no, I'd never use you like that. Treat you as a conquest or to tick a box off."

Why wouldn't she? While Remy should be used to Amelia saying things she has no context for, she's not. "But everyone wants something from me, wants *that* from me?"

Amelia shrugs with a smile. "Not me, my time isn't transactional. Even if you never cooked or did anything for me I'd still enjoy your company because you're you."

And now Remy really doesn't know what to do. She'll cook until she can figure it out.

Amelia is just there as Remy cleans and starts a pot boiling. While the water boils, she takes stock of the snow fridge. She gets a pasta dough going with the spinach that needs to be used. Amelia puts on music and Remy starts singing along without thinking about it.

"No one ever calls me great, or says so many nice things about me. Well, I suppose about my food? Bon Appetite had an article recently, I was one of the chefs interviewed. They said a lot of really nice things about my food. But no one says nice things about me. I'm a brash, abrasive arsehole people tolerate because of my food."

Amelia casually leans against the counter arms crossed. "Don't get me wrong, your food is incredible, but you're pretty incredible, too. That's not something I feel obligated to say, or I'm ignoring warning signs. You're a good person who makes good food."

Remy dishes the food up and takes time to put the plates together properly before presenting them. Amelia's mouth drops. "It's so pretty I don't want to eat it," she whispers as she takes a picture. "I need to show Mama, I don't think I can describe this…"

Then she cuddles into Remy and takes a selfie of the two of them. "I want to remember everything, not just the food."

Amelia takes a small bite and tears well up. She chews slowly, eyes closed and swallows, she takes a deep breath waving the tears away. "Oh my god, Remy," she sips her water, blinking back more tears. "Oh fuck," Amelia takes another small bite tears streaming down her cheeks. "Remy," she sobs out swallowing.

Remy's heard about people reduced to tears by food but doesn't think she's seen it in person before. She reaches out and takes Amelia's hand, then picks up her fork and takes a bite with the other. She can ignore everything she should have done instead focusing on how emotional Amelia is and how nice it is to be sitting with her.

Amelia takes a deep breath, waving away the tears. "Oh wow, oh," she leans over, kissing Remy. "God bless it, you are so ridiculously talented. I've never—I don't know if I can express what I'm feeling in words, and my job is assigning words to feelings."

"Let me make it again when I have the right ingredients," Remy murmurs blushing.

"Oh, I can't imagine this getting better, I—" she shakes her head and shrugs, tears dripping down her cheeks again.

Remy shifts closer and wraps her arms around Amelia, holding her as she cries and takes another bite. "I've never seen someone reduced to tears by my food before."

"Can you make this for Mama? I want her to experience this."

Remy nods. "I can try, or I can make her something else? I just want her to like me and my food as much as you seem to," Remy admits softly, throat closing and stomach tightening. Surely this will be the time she is laughed at and ridiculed.

Amelia swallows and takes a deep breath releasing it purposefully. "She's going to love you, Remzie."

There are those pesky feelings and the immediate drive to be an absolute wanker to push Amelia and anyone else away. Hurt them before they can hurt her.

"Tell that little voice to fuck off. You're worthy of love and kindness, Remy Kensington."

"I almost believe it when you say it, not just the accent, the everything about you, if we're being honest. But there's this irrational fear it's going to get bad if I let myself connect with someone."

Amelia cuddles into Remy, taking another bite. "Want to talk about what that means?"

Remy shrugs leaning against Amelia, enjoying the connection.

Amelia takes another bite, savouring it, fine to wait for whatever Remy wants to do.

"I think I could with you? But it's like the words are stuck and I can't get them to un-stick for anyone."

Amelia nods, swallowing. "That's understandable. If you want to try some resources to see if we can get them to un-stick we can, but it's also okay to let them shake loose on their own. I'll be here, if you want me to be."

"Really?" Remy manages.

Amelia turns slightly and takes Remy's hand. "Yeah, really, I want to keep in touch. We can FaceTime and cook together, or more accurately you can cook and I'll watch you," she blushes. "I really like to watch you cook. The way you float around the kitchen. How you can do so many things at once. The cute little facial expressions you make. I like it. I don't know, I'm glad we're stuck together."

"Same. This has been nice, and you're making being stuck a bit more bearable."

Amelia sighs. "I'm gonna make myself sick if I eat anymore, but I want to keep eating. Can we save this? I want to eat the rest later or tomorrow for breakfast."

Remy nods. "I can't either, but I want to, for the first time in as long as I can remember."

"Good! That's good. Okay, let me grab a to-go box and we can pack these up."

Amelia stands up, goes to dry storage, and comes back with takeaway tins. "Ah, takeaway tins, good idea."

Amelia giggles and nods as she takes the leftovers and puts them away in the snow fridge.

"What would you like to do?" Amelia asks, walking back over to Remy.

Remy's knee-jerk reaction is to say something snarky, but she shrugs instead.

"Can we cuddle and snug in the flour fort?" Amelia asks.

Remy's brow furrows. "Snug?"

"Isn't that what you called making out?"

"Oh, no, snog, yeah, I think I'd like that actually," she

blushes. "I've never done this nor wanted to do this with anyone. I'm still not sure how to feel about everything I'm feeling."

"We can talk, or not talk about it, whenever you want."

Instead of talking, Remy opts for not talking. She gently kisses Amelia, helping her down into the flour fort. Enjoying the way Amelia curls up against her and sighs.

12

Remy doesn't remember falling asleep, she and Amelia did some grounding techniques before bed to help with the nightmares, then they chatted more and must have fallen asleep. For the first time in as long as Remy can remember, she doesn't have nightmares. Amelia's techniques helped. Everything Amelia does and suggests helps, though.

Amelia cuddles into Remy's chest deeper and hums. "Morning," she murmurs.

"I didn't have nightmares," Remy whispers, still unsure if she's really awake, if this isn't part of the dream still.

"Good, I'm glad the exercises helped, Remzie."

"Everything you do helps, Doc," Remy says, hugging Amelia closer.

Amelia's face scrunches in a cute way with a little shrug. "I'm kind of good at my job, I'll let Mama brag."

Remy chuckles. "I suspect you saying that is like me saying it. I'm going to dip to the loo, I'll be back."

Amelia nods. "I need to go, too. Help me up?"

Remy helps pull Amelia up out of the flour fort and she hugs Remy. "I can't wait for Mama to meet you. If you want to go to Mama's?"

Remy nods. "What if she doesn't like me? No one ever

likes me…"

"Mama will, already does. Everyone is going to love you and your cooking because you're lovable and interesting."

"I don't think I'll ever get used to the thought someone may not hate my company," Remy admits before ducking into the loo quickly to avoid sobbing like an infant.

After finishing her business and rinsing her mouth out, she shifts back out of the bathroom and looks around the deserted diner. The snow has stopped falling, or at least slowed? Remy wants to eat, find something to use as a shovel, and start digging to Ruby's. Amelia comes out of the back tears streaming down her cheeks. "Somehow it's as good, if not better cold?" she manages through her tears.

Remy takes a bite of the cold noodles. "Oh, that is good."

"I want everyone else to try this too, if that's okay?"

Remy nods. "Or I can make something else?"

Amelia shakes her head tears still rushing down her cheeks. "No, they need to experience this, Remy, I don't think you understand the—I still don't have words to express what's happening to me when I eat this."

"The dreadfully awkward woman that just wants to make people happy with her food wants to cry too," Remy admits. "No one likes my savoury food this much."

"Have they not tried your savoury food? Everything you've made is so good. And listen, this isn't a culinary metropolis, but I live in the West Loop back home, I can walk to at least three Michelin rated restaurants."

Remy shrugs fidgeting and can't get anything clever or quippy out.

Amelia puts the tin down and takes Remy's cheeks gently in the way she does and kisses her tenderly before resting their foreheads together. "Seriously, no one can eat anything you make and not like it. There's a reason you have six James

Beard awards and almost got a star. Do you ever cook like this for anyone back home?"

Remy shakes her head and shrugs again, taking a deep breath. "Sorry," she stops fighting the tears. "Sorry, erm, no, seldomly I suppose."

"Would you ever do something savoury at your restaurant?"

Remy shakes her head. "Once, won't make that mistake again." She can't think about that without returning to the kitchen, so she shuts it down immediately, trying to focus on the way Amelia's hands feel instead.

She shifts how she's standing and kisses Remy, helping to ground her further here instead of there. "I'm sorry," she murmurs against Remy's lips. "Need to do some breathing exercises?"

Remy shakes her head slightly. "Keep doing this," she responds, focusing on all the various sensations kissing can evoke.

Amelia starts to lean into the kiss and stops herself almost as fast leaning back.

"Okay, as much as I want to keep doing this with you we should eat and start digging," Amelia murmurs breathlessly, cheeks flushed.

"Yes, okay," Remy clears her throat. "I rather enjoying doing this with you."

"Stay instead of going home and we'll cuddle and kiss as much as you want."

Remy chuckles. "Tempting."

The scary thing is a tiny part of her would drop everything to stay here with someone she's only known for a couple of days. Before she can push Amelia away and try to sabotage everything, she takes another bite of cold noodles. "Do you want this or should I whip up a scramble like yesterday morning?"

"Oh, I want both, but I'm happy to eat these cold and have a piece of pie. I want to eat anything you make, I'm in awe of your talent, and I'm not saying that because of everything, it's the truth. I don't lie either."

Remy blushes. "Stop making the dreadfully awkward woman so happy, she may end up taking you up on the offer to stay and you'd be stuck with me."

"Couldn't imagine anything better than being stuck with you, Remzie," Amelia responds, taking another bite and fighting tears. "Sorry, I'm going to be ridiculous and cry with every bite of this. I seriously… Oh," she sighs and shrugs.

Remy can't keep sitting in all the feelings, she gets a banana and eats it while searching for something to shovel with. There's a large metal salad bowl that has bits of food dried to it. She doesn't have to wash it, she can shovel with it. Remy opens the back door and looks at their makeshift snow fridge. Then carefully moves the food to one side and carefully starts digging out the other. Shovelling bowls full of snow off to the side, or at least trying to, it's not working. Remy has never shovelled before, so admittedly she doesn't know what she's doing.

"Why don't we try shovelling some of the snow into the sink?" Amelia suggests.

Remy tries and it helps, she's making progress. Amelia tearfully takes bites while shovelling with a smaller bowl.

Remy smiles at Amelia. "Want to sit with that? I can handle this."

"No, I've enjoyed our snowcation, but this is the longest I've been away from Mama since I moved back. I know the aunties can take care of her but I'm worried."

Remy nods.

"Lia, that you?" comes Georgia's grating voice. "Sounds like you're crying. Are you okay?"

"Yes! We're digging out the back of the snow fridge we

made. Remy made dinner last night and it's so good I keep crying, you gotta try a bite!"

"Glad it's just food making you cry…"

"Rest assured I've tried to be on my best behaviour," Remy says.

A hole forms and Remy can see Georgia, the doughy bottle blonde, with a gentleman that looks like Father Christmas.

He says something laughing and his accent is so thick Remy can't even pretend to understand anything he said.

"Yes, Bubba, this is Remy, Remy this is Ruby's husband, Bubba," Amelia says, gesturing between the two as she speaks.

"Lovely to meet you, Bubba, thank you both for the help shovelling, it's tricky with salad bowls."

Bubba says something and Remy feels like an absolute idiot. "Sorry, I can't understand you."

He laughs and waves it off, then takes a deep breath and talks slower as if that will help, and it sort of does? She thinks she recognises something about cooking.

"Ah, yes, perhaps before we start the trek to Mama's house?"

Bubba nods and mumbles something with a warm smile.

"Wait, try these noodles, they're as good cold as they are off the stove."

Georgia obliges and takes a bite, she instantly tears up too. "Oh wow, you wasn't jokin'," she murmurs.

Bubba takes a bite too and nods, his rough, ruddy face melting into a smile and mumbles something softly.

"Thank you, erm, it's just something I threw together with what we had, it's better with the right ingredients."

"Ain't no way to make this better, Remy, you's damn good at this. There any pie left? I wanna see if it's really better than Mama's," Georgia asks smiling.

"Yeah, I saved some for you all to try."

Bubba mumbles something slowly, pointing to the noodles.

Amelia nods. "Agreed, Ruby has to try this. I've been trying not to eat it all, I want everyone to try it. Isn't it just, there aren't words?"

"Really aren't," Georgia agrees.

They walk through the back of the makeshift fridge and Bubba laughs, pulling his shirt back over his rotund belly.

"Remy was worried about the perishables. Come on, the pie is in here. We can have a piece with coffee. Y'all got coffee?"

Georgia nods. "Bubba here's a genius, got everything workin', heat and all."

"We've been using the oven to keep things warm-ish over here and cuddling," Amelia says, blushing.

"So Remy's good at cookin', kissin', and cuddlin'?" Georgia quips in a teasing tone gently nudging Amelia.

"Stop." Amelia's blush deepens and she playfully bats Georgia. "She's good at everything, we've been having fun over here."

They take the pie and noodles over to the house which reminds Remy of the carriage house Viktor and Helga had on the estate. Ruby is Amelia's height and about as wide as she is tall, salt and pepper hair held down by years of oven grease. She's in the kitchen getting coffee poured. "I'm so glad you two are okay! How's the diner, any cracks or leaks?"

"Things are doing okay, we didn't notice any," Amelia responds, smiling.

Bubba adds something Remy can't understand, but Ruby does and she hugs Remy and Amelia. "Thanks you two for thinking of me and trying to protect the food. Now, what's got you all red and puffy?"

"Remy's food, try these," Amelia responds. And there's

another person crying over her food. She hugs Remy, Remy awkwardly hugs back.

"In all my years." She takes a deep breath and another bite. They quietly stand in the kitchen eating the leftover dinner with tears running along their cheeks.

"Wait, you gotta share that with Mama," Georgia says, sniffling and wiping her face on the back of her hand.

Remy watches as Amelia, Georgia, Bubba, and Ruby transition to the pie. Everyone moans and Ruby cries harder.

"My stars, how many of these you made child?" she asks.

"This was the first time! I didn't even give her a recipe, just a list of ingredients. Oh, and look how pretty the plates were last night!" Amelia takes her phone out and pulls up the picture of them hugging then flips to the plates.

Georgia gasps. "How'd you make something so pretty over at Ruby's?"

Remy isn't sure what to do with all the praise she's getting. "Goodness, erm," she clears her throat. "Sorry, all I want to do is make people happy with my food... Thank you all, I only threw some things together, this is nothing impressive."

Ruby puts her fork down and takes Remy's hands in hers. "Darlin' the fact you got this," she gestures to the noodle box and pie tin. "Outta my kitchen is a miracle. You are truly talented. This is a gift. God's given you a gift and I'm so happy I got to experience that gift."

Wow, those words hit differently when coming from someone old enough to be Remy's parent. This validation is something she'd typically never get from someone that age.

Remy shrugs and manages a wan smile, eyes cast down to her feet. These people may not be safe, she can't turn into a blubbering child and invite ridicule.

Ruby's callused, beige hands gently cup Remy's cheeks and she lifts her gaze so they're making eye contact. "Darling, you hear me and know how talented you are, right? How incredible what you did here is?" Oh dear, she's as sincere as Amelia, it's getting harder to keep her composure.

Don't you dare cry you talentless cunt, or I'll really give you something to cry about.

"See?" Amelia says softly. "Not just me saying it, they see it too."

Remy nods slightly. "I forgot my phone, excuse me…"

Cry harder, Piggy.

She gets outside and back to the diner before the tears start. Amelia doesn't let her stay alone, she catches up to Remy and hugs her.

"Tell the little voice to fuck off, Remzie."

Remy can't keep falling apart like this, she's better than this. She takes a deep breath, trying to push the emotions back. "It's different to hear those words from someone their age," she pushes out, taking deep breaths.

"You're gonna get an earful of how talented you are and good your food is at Mama's."

"I'm not sure what to do with all the praise. No one has screamed at me or called me worthless in days. There's no one critiquing me, even when I use ingredients that are about to go off and dried bulk herbs. I can't help wondering what you want, what they'll want, in return for the kindness. What I'll have to put up with…"

Amelia hugs her tighter, gently rubbing her back.
"Nothing except for you to recognise how incredible you are."

"But—"

"No buts, buttercup, we just want to thank you for coming into our lives, no matter for how long, and sharing your talent with us."

Remy takes a deep breath and pushes it out. "Should we make lunch before gearing up, or eat at your mama's?"

"Oh, we may want to take some staples? I don't remember what the fridge looks like... Wait, no, it's a holiday weekend, I'm sure there's plenty. We should be fine?"

"Okay, maybe just to be safe I'll pack something to make late lunch when we get over there. Did you have enough? What do we need to do before we start our hike?"

"For you to eat something? A banana and a bite of noodles aren't enough..."

Remy smiles at Amelia, trying to be reassuring. "Promise I'll eat when we get to your mama's."

Amelia bites her lip, concern etched across her soft features. "I don't want you to faint walking over..."

"Darling, sometimes I work eighteen hours without a break. I can handle a five minute walk."

"Please? Not a forcing thing, an I care thing,"

Remy wants to be a wanker, but as with everything Amelia-related, just lets out a heavy sigh and nods fidgeting with her curls. "Very well."

"Thank you. Want me to make you something? I can, um, pour cereal?"

Remy laughs and shakes her head. "No, thank you."

Walking by the snow fridge, she glances at what's on her diet, she can't keep deviating. She grabs a carrot and celery stalk on the way out of the diner. Taking a deep breath of the bitter air and a bite of celery.

"Thanks, Remzie, I appreciate it. Will you eat at Mama's too?"

Remy nods. "Promise, I'll try what I make for you all. Are there any allergies?"

"Doctors have Mama on a special diet that's supposed to help with the Chemo and cancer. No red meat or pork, minimally processed foods, lots of fruits and veggies. If Auntie June made it she's diabetic. But nothing else I'm aware of?"

"Okay, that shouldn't be a problem. Should we ask Ruby and Bubba before taking food?"

Amelia shakes her head. "Ruby was ready to make me a bag Friday. We can't take the store but let's grab some staples."

It doesn't take long to pack a small bag with staples and the personal items Remy and Amelia nearly left at the diner. Remy changes out of the track suit and into the suit she'd been wearing on the plane. She feels a little better showing up at someone's home in clothes that fit and don't smell like she's been living in them for days. They walk back inside Ruby's house and Remy offers another wan smile. "Want me to whip you up something before we leave for Mrs Haskins'?"

"Yes, but if you do, we may end up handing you the keys and retiring. You're God's gift to food."

Bubba's nodding and mumbling something that may be about food but Remy honestly isn't sure.

"Well, erm, goodness, thank you," Remy says instead of running away sobbing. She must get the weakness under control before returning to work or she'll be asking for a smack.

"Make us something later. I imagine you need to get home to Mama?"

Amelia nods blushing. "Intellectually I understand she's fine with the aunties but I'm worried—"

"No, we understand. Remy promise to come back before you leave town?" Ruby says as Georgia is saying something similar.

Remy nods. "I'll cook something up for you all before I

leave, promise."
"Bubba got the other ATV out, should make it easier to get over there."
"Thank you, we'll bring it back, promise."
Remy and Amelia trudge out into the garage and Remy looks at the quad bike and bites her lip. "Can you drive quad bikes? I never learned."
Amelia grins. "Oh yeah, Georgia and I got up to good trouble with the cousins on these. Hop on and hold on."
Remy obliges, putting a cycling helmet on, before wrapping her arms around Amelia's waist.
They wave at Georgia, Bubba, and Ruby as Amelia guns the engine and takes off over the snow.

13

Remy is a pile of nerves as they pull into the drive and stop the quad bike. She gets off and wonders if it's too late to run to the nearest airport. Unsure she can handle meeting a parent, regardless of whether it's a friend's or otherwise.

Amelia leans over and kisses Remy's cheek, squeezing her hand lightly. "Deep breaths, everyone is going to love you because you are lovable. Tell that little voice to fuck off, okay?"

Remy nods incapable of actually saying anything. Amelia laces her fingers through Remy's and they trudge up to the house. The door opens and the woman standing there looks exactly like Amelia, only older.

"Hiya Auntie! How's Mama?" Amelia asks.

"Doin' good sugar, been takin' it easy and spendin' time with our stories. Is this the famous Remy?"

Remy blushes. "Infamous perhaps, Remy Kensington, lovely to meet you."

"Ooo girl, listen to that, like honey, say something else."

Typically, those comments make Remy bristle but not here. "Anything you want, Mrs Oh, erm, I suppose you're not Mrs Haskins too. What shall I call you?"

She giggles. "Suppose it would be Mrs Johnson, if we're

goin' that route. Now my sister said you're some fancy chef?"

Amelia nods. "Her food is incredible, dinner last night made me cry, then somehow it was better this morning? I don't have much, but I needed you each to have a bite. I also saved some pie, but we need Remy to make another one."

"Sounds like we need to play in the kitchen, Remy?"

Remy isn't sure what to do, she nods slightly. "Sounds lovely. I want to make everyone lunch, if I may? A bite of noodles and pie won't do."

"Can't wait," she loops an arm through Remy's and walks her into the house. The group of women in the kitchen could be clones of each other. "Look who made it! Remy's offering to whip us up some lunch."

"Well, it's wonderful to meet you in person, Remy! I'm Amelia's mother, Mrs Haskins, I've been wanting to do this since we first talked."

She envelops Remy in a hug, squeezing in a way no one's held her before and she may start sobbing.

"Welcome darlin', I'm so glad to have you here," that does it, Remy cracks.

Piggy and her unbecoming feelings.

"Sorry," Remy manages, trying to swallow the tears.
"Let it out, safe space to…"

Pity party because nobody loves her.

Remy needs to stop crying and cook, but no part of her wants to break out of the comfort of the hug. She should though, she can't get used to this—

As if she can hear the inner thoughts, Amelia comes up behind Remy and hugs her whispering, "Tell the little voice to f-off Remzie."

Remy chuckle sobs. "No more—"

"Not in Mama's house! That's like swearing in church," Amelia says with an endearing giggle and blush that makes it easier to get the emotions back in the box they belong in.

"Right, I'll be on my best behaviour, promise. Oh," she takes a deep breath. "Sorry that wasn't very—"

"Never apologise for crying or expressing yourself, dear. You're allowed to do both here. Need to hug a little longer?" Mrs Haskins asks in a tone that is similar to Amelia's just huskier.

"I'm afraid I may never get anything done if you and your daughter keep offering to hug me. Thank you, sorry, my parents aren't very warm, I didn't realise how nice that could be."

"Well, that breaks my heart," Mrs Freeman says and gathers Remy up. Her therapist would be proud that she's fighting the urge to be a wanker and push everyone away.

"Oh goodness, your family has a gift," Remy murmurs and clears her throat. "Why don't you share the noodles and I'll get to this. Are you really okay with me taking over your kitchen, Mrs Haskins?"

Everyone has a bite of noodle in their mouth and tears pouring down their cheeks. "Oh child, you gotta gift, this is... You made this at Ruby's?"

Remy nods and rubs her neck. "It's really nothing—"

"I am seventy years old and never once has food reduced me to tears. Don't discount your talent because someone made you feel small," Mrs Johnson says wiping at the tears rolling down her cheeks.

Remy blushes. "Thank you, Mrs Johnson, I'm trying."

"All anyone will ever ask is you try. Now this here is the pie?"

Amelia nods. "I didn't even give her a recipe, only a list of ingredients."

The women take forks from Amelia and take a bite.

"Lord in heaven, you really never made chess pie before?"

"She's not calling you a liar, just can't believe this is your first," Amelia offers with that supportive smile of hers.

This kitchen is tidy, Remy doesn't have to clean before she cooks. She shrugs. "I love the challenge of figuring out a new recipe. Chess Pie is like custard tarts, so I took what I know and applied it to this, it's nothing, really."

Mrs Freeman rolls her eyes and shakes her head.

"So you're like our girl here and discount your talents. 'Auntie, it's just an APA Distinguished Scientific Award for an Early Career Contribution to Psychology don't make such a fuss'," she says in a hilarious impression of Amelia.

Remy laughs. "Yes, Amelia mentioned she'd let you all brag about her accomplishments and the letters after her name. In the couple of days I've sat with her, she's done more to help me than years of therapy and unhealthy coping mechanisms."

"Oh, so she didn't tell you—" and that begins the three women gushing over Amelia, and Amelia downplaying everything. Seeing Amelia take the piss in an endearing way, not traumatic like it always is for Remy, is heartwarming.

Remy gets the plates and puts them together properly using what she has in the small kitchen. Once the plates are finished, she gets the table set and presents the dishes.

Amelia is already in tears. "They're so beautiful, Remy."

Remy bites her lip, fidgeting. "You and your family deserve something beautiful, I—"

Amelia stops her with a chaste kiss. "Was about to discount how remarkable you are, please stop doing that."

"But you might stop kissing me," Remy responds, blushing.

"Lord, it's so beautiful I almost don't want to eat it, never in all my years. Someone get a picture, please? I want to put it in the family thread. They're going to be so jealous we got snowed in here," Mrs Johnson says carefully shifting how she's standing so she can study the plate from a different angle.

"You're going to eat, right?" Amelia asks.

Remy nods and shows off her salad. "I'll try yours, but I made this for myself. Promised I'd make something I could eat too."

"Honey, you are too skinny to be eating rabbit food," Mrs Haskins says, tutting her tongue.

Remy blushes and glances down fidgeting with her salad fork.

Amelia says something Remy can't understand, but the older women look at her with sympathy and nods responding.

Mrs Johnson hugs Remy. "I'm sorry so many people were so awful to you, darlin'. You didn't deserve any of that."

Remy melts into the hug slightly. "A slight part of me is starting to believe that."

"Well, we'll keep saying it until all your parts do."

Surprisingly, a video call comes in, Remy answers. "Hello?"

Kona's heart-shaped obsidian face pops up and she appears relieved. "Oh thank god, I've been so worried! Where are you?"

Remy's brow furrows, surprised by how concerned Kona seems. "Oh, erm, stuck in the states, snow—"

"I know!" she interrupts. "The good 'Lord' was being a right cunt about it, I smacked him, sorry. Like seriously though, because your family probably won't ask me around again," she pauses taking a deep breath and pushing it out, waving at her warm brown eyes. "Sorry, I've been a mess.

When I saw the news… I tried calling and texting," her voice catches and she's swiping at her eyes again. "Remy, I don't know what I'd do if something happened to you."

Remy's never seen Kona so emotive and didn't think she cared for her much. "Oh, well, wow," she clears her throat. "I've had a lovely family over here take me in—"

Amelia comes up behind Remy and leans down, waving at Kona with a warm smile. "She cooked for us and we really want to keep her."

"Oh, isn't she so talented?" Kona responds excitedly. "I keep telling her she needs to open her own place, but she never listens. I'm Kona, Remy's… Oh, erm, well, you know, I spend time with her when she's not in the kitchen or gym."

Amelia smirks side eyeing Remy. "The way Remy talks she's always in the kitchen or gym."

"She is." Kona chuckles and takes another breath blinking back tears. "But she's quite wonderful, so even if all I get is a couple hours a month, I take it. Are you seriously okay? The way it's being covered over here sounds truly terrible."

Remy bites her lip and fidgets with a bit of salad. "It was rather harrowing—I, erm, I almost died. A bobby found me after my rental ended up in a drift. The doctor and I were stranded in a diner and only just made it to her mums. She's been taking excellent care of me."

"Thank you, doctor!" Kona says to Amelia before turning back to Remy. "Seriously, please be careful and safe. When you get home, can I see you for more than twenty minutes, please?"

Amelia nods and puts her hands on Remy's shoulders. "She's about to say something snarky to push you away, but I won't let her, she'd love to, Kona. If we don't talk her into staying here and taking over Ruby's, her food has made me cry on multiple occasions."

"If you do, I'll come too, I can be a writer anywhere," Kona responds with a slight chuckle, blushing.

Remy isn't sure what's happening, but she doesn't hate it. She bites her lip, fidgeting more with her salad. "We should go here, I threw together a quick coq au vin for them." Remy turns the camera so she can show off the plates. Mrs Haskins and Amelia's aunties wave at the phone.

"You're welcome anytime too, sugar," Mrs Haskins says.

"Oh my, aren't you stunning, and that accent," Mrs Johnson says, causing both Kona and Remy to blush.

Remy flips the camera back and Kona is chuckling.

"Thank you, goodness, don't go praising Remy like that, she'll run for the hills."

"While she downplays it and tells you to f-off," Amelia says in her terrible impression of Remy's accent, laughing. "Yeah, she's finally hearing us. Maybe she can finally hear you too?"

"Amelia is an award-winning therapist, probably the best kind of doctor for me to be stuck with," Remy says now she can finally get the words out. She's not sure why seeing Kona is impacting her like this. Perhaps she didn't realise how much she missed her, even though they're nothing serious?

Kona grins showing off her perfect gap tooth smile and shrugs slightly. "I'm glad you're with someone that knows how to talk to you. Amelia and family, her coq au vin is my favourite and always makes me want to cry." She chuckles at herself and glances up at Amelia. "Remy's seriously so good at everything in the kitchen, enjoy your time with her." She shifts her gaze to Remy. "Have fun and be safe. Call if you need anything. I can't really do anything, but I'm here and worried. Love you, bye!" she panics, waving as if trying to bat the words away. "Wait, no, I didn't mean to say the L word. I like you an appropriate amount, bye." She blushes and ends the call.

Remy stares at the blank screen for a moment unable to

shake the surprise. "That's Kona—I didn't think she liked me that much," she finds herself saying out loud.

"See? You probably have more people than you think that care about you and would miss you if something had happened," Amelia says softly, giving Remy a hug before sitting down.

"I think I'd like to… Can we eat? I don't know how to feel about what just happened."

Amelia nods. "Absolutely, and if you need to process out loud, we're happy to hold space, no judgement."

Remy intellectually believes what Amelia is saying but can't help the years of trauma.

Amelia leans over, resting their foreheads together. "Tell that little voice to f-off. You're a good person with people that care about you, we will not weaponise our approval or support."

Remy nods and sips the water that somehow appeared in front of her.

"God bless this meal and everyone around our table, amen." Everyone takes their first bite and it's a symphony of contentment. "Bless us, Lord, thank you for bringing Remy into our lives!" She looks over at Remy. "You are one talented young woman."

"I'm so glad we spent so long arguing about what to eat because it gave us a chance to experience this," Mrs Haskins says, smiling at Remy.

"You are so good at this," Amelia murmurs, blinking back tears.

Remy takes a small bite from Amelia's plate. "Oh, that isn't bad, I should have—"

"Nothing could make this better," Mrs Johnson interjects. "Oh, this is food that deserves to be worshipped! God, thank you for blessing Remy. Thank you for her undeniable talent and for diverting her plane and bringing her into our lives.

Amen."

Remy takes a bite of her salad and it's good too. It would have been better with fresh ingredients, but it's easier to eat than what she made everyone else.

Mrs Johnson's phone rings. "Ma, what's that in the picture? Who's cookin' like that?"

She smiles at the camera, swallowing a bite. "Remy, your cousin brought her home from Ruby's, they were stuck there. It's every bit as good as it looks."

"If we dig out is there enough for us? Because I've never seen food so pretty."

"I promised to cook for everyone before going home. If I go home, everyone here keeps hugging me and telling me how good my food is. I may have to stay instead of going back to West London," Remy responds.

"Yeah, stay here and make magic food for us. We'll give you all the hugs and compliments."

Remy laughs. "Tempting."

"Auntie, you and Remy gonna cook?"

Mrs Haskins nods. "Absolutely. Y'all get out and over we'll do a proper Sunday dinner."

"Love y'all, but I want to get back to my food. Come on by, any time. Be safe and take your time."

14

Mrs Haskins smiles warmly and leans back away from the plate taking a sip of water. "What'll it take to get you to stick around here, Remy? Doesn't have to be forever, just long enough for us to enjoy more of your God given talent."

Remy should run fast and far, before things get bad, they always get bad. But in the time she's been with Amelia it hasn't been bad, she's been nothing but supportive and kind and understanding.

"As terrifying as it is, a small part of me wants to throw everything away and stay here making food that makes people happy."

"I'll hug you as often as you want?" Amelia offers.

"And we can play in the kitchen whenever you want. Maybe I teach you some of Gran's recipes? I tried to teach Amelia but she—"

"Nearly burnt the house down," Amelia interjects. "I think I told you? I am good at a lot of things, unfortunately cooking isn't one of them."

"Wait, you really want to share family recipes with me?" Remy asks softly.

Mrs Haskins nods with a warm smile. "Nothing would make me happier, baby girl. If you want, you don't have to, of course."

Remy can't help but wrap her arms around the woman, squeezing tighter than she probably should. "It would be an honour, thank you," she whispers when she's sure she won't start bawling.

"No, thank you! I'm excited," Mrs Haskins yawns. "Oof, sorry, think I may need a lie down. After I'm up, we can play in the kitchen together."

Remy nods still swallowing her tears, she swipes at her eyes quickly. "I'd like that very much, thank you."

Mrs Haskins gives Remy one more hug before she starts towards what Remy is assuming is her bedroom.

"A lie down sounds good. I cried so much over the beauty of these flavours I done wore myself out," Mrs Johnson adds.

The older women all shuffle out, leaving Remy and Amelia in the kitchen together.

"I really like your family," Remy murmurs.

"And they really like you. Mama's been sad not having anyone to share her recipes with. She tried with me but I'm just no good in the kitchen. Lane has zero interest in anything domestic. Thank you so much for being the person she needs."

"I'm honoured she wants to share something so sacred with me. I'm just—"

"About to be mean to yourself. You're pretty great and worthy of our recipes. They're passed down through the years, your mama told you, you told your kids."

Remy is having a harder time swallowing the feelings. These aren't just her mother's recipes, they're generational. Amelia shifts so she's holding Remy. "You're allowed to express your feelings, or swallow them. Want to cuddle on the couch with a movie, or I can show you my book collection?"

"Both sound lovely," Remy murmurs. "I'm terrified and want to run away, don't let me."

Amelia hugs Remy a little tighter, rubbing her back. "Thank you for trusting me enough to admit that. Promise I won't."

Remy wants to add more, spill all her secrets and everything weighing her down, but she can't get the words out. "I don't care if we sit and read or sit with a movie. I never thought I'd enjoy cuddling so much."

Amelia leans back. "Sounds like Kona would cuddle with you, if you end up back home?" she says with a mischievous, lopsided grin.

Remy can't help but chuckle. The thought of cuddling with Kona sends a warm fuzzy feeling through Remy's stomach and chest she doesn't really understand. "She's nice, I didn't think she cared about me."

Amelia nods with an understanding smile. "Sounds like she genuinely enjoys your company and will take whatever time and energy you can give her. Which sounds like your speed, yeah?"

"Perhaps?" she waffles for a beat but finally adds, "I think you're my speed, Doc, which terrifies me."

Amelia takes Remy's hands in hers. "Remzie, I promise regardless of what our relationship looks like I will do my best to never hurt you or make you feel worthless. I want to support and empower you to make the best choices for you."

Remy bites the inside of her cheek and swallows her tears. "Thanks," she manages.

"Let's start with a movie on the couch, you look like you could use one of Mama's blankets and to cuddle."

Remy lets Amelia lead her into a cosy living room. Amelia picks up a large fluffy blanket and wraps it around them. The couch is obscenely comfortable, Remy feels like she's melting into it.

"This couch'll suck you in if you're not careful," Amelia playfully warns.

"I may fall asleep," Remy murmurs. She never sleeps like this, or has so much downtime.

"If you do, I got you, you're safe. Need to do some grounding exercises?"

Remy shrugs and curls into Amelia. "I'm safe with you, your family is safe, I'll be okay. What movie are we going to watch?"

"I'm not sure, but some trashy holiday movie with no stakes?"

"Sounds grand."

Remy doesn't remember falling asleep but she wakes with a start curled up on the couch holding Amelia. Another auntie is taking a picture.

"Sorry, didn't mean to wake you, two of you just look so cute together," she turns the phone around showing a couple pictures, they're exceptionally good.

"Oh my, you took those with a camera phone? They're remarkable."

She waves it off. "Just a fun little thing I do."

"Would you mind? Can you send that to me? I'd love a copy, Mrs—"

"Oh please don't missus me, I've always hated that. Just call me Rose."

"Copy of what?" Amelia murmurs, curling deeper into Remy's chest.

"Your auntie, Rose, took some pretty remarkable photos of us."

"Yeah, she's won a ton of awards, she's like the Julia Childs of nature photography."

"So we're all downplaying our accomplishments then, got it," Remy chuckles.

Rose waves it off and shows Amelia the picture. "See, it's just a little phone picture, nothing to get excited over."

"Aw, we look adorable." Amelia glances back at Remy. "Sorry I fell asleep on you, I don't remember falling asleep."

"Neither do I. This couch is awfully comfortable. If Mama doesn't want us sharing a room, I'll happily sleep on this couch."

"Lord knows you deserve a little fun, Bedelia, I'm sure it'll be fine," Rose quips with a wink and smile.

Amelia blushes and sputters.

Remy laughs. "She won't sleep with me because I'm not okay, and it would be unethical, so we cuddle and occasionally kiss."

Amelia blushes deeper and nods.

Rose laughs and puts her arms around Remy and Amelia. "Hopefully, you'll get to a place where you are okay. Have a good rest?"

Remy nods and leans into the contact slightly. "I've never slept as well as I do when cuddling with your niece. She's the safest I remember feeling."

Remy doesn't mean to be honest, she means to take the piss, but she can't take it back.

Amelia smiles. "I like and appreciate you, Remzie, I sleep really well with you too."

"Yeah, I like and appreciate you too, Bedelia."

Amelia laughs. "No, no, you can't start calling me that too, it's not supposed to stick," she laughs harder.

"I don't know Doctor Amelia Bedelia has a nice ring to it," Remy teases, chuckling.

Mrs Haskins comes walking in with a steaming mug smiling warmly.

"At the very least you'll come out of this lifelong friends. Since we all had a good rest, what do you say we play in the kitchen a little? Sunday dinner isn't gonna cook itself and I'd love to show you some of my great-great-grandma's recipes?"

Remy can't be a sobbing mess when someone says something nice or wants to spend time with her. She blinks back tears and nods, unsure she can actually say anything.

Mrs Haskins gathers her up and hugs her tight. "Need to let those out or to ignore them and cook?" she asks softly.

"Cook," Remy manages without crying, she blinks away more tears.

"Okay." She gives Remy one more big squeeze before standing up, almost using Remy as an aid. "Usually keep everything on hand for this, it's a Sunday staple. I'm so excited to share it with you! Bedelia, are you going to keep us company and play DJ?"

Amelia rolls her eyes and chuckles, shaking her head. "Not if you keep calling me that. Actually, that's a lie. I love watching you both in the kitchen, I can't wait to see what you can do together."

They move back into the kitchen, Mrs Haskins has an arm around Remy and there's something deeply comforting, not panic inducing about it.

"Now these recipes are passed down kitchen to kitchen, I'm the first one to write them down. When I first got sick, I didn't want anything to happen to them should anything happen to me. Can you do me a favour?"

Remy nods. "Of course, anything, you and your daughter have been such a tremendous help."

"This is a big ask, you can back out if you want. Amelia can't cook and Lane probably couldn't even find the kitchen, can you help Amelia with these after I'm gone?"

Remy's stomach is in her throat. "Really?" she manages.

Mrs Haskins nods and takes Remy's hands in hers. "Very much so, yes, please? If you can and want to, no pressure."

Remy nods slightly and breaks.

Come now, squeal for us, Piggy.

Amelia and Mrs Haskins are hugging Remy as she's trying and failing to pull herself together.

"Tell that little voice to f-off Remzie."

"Sorry, sorry, I'm not usually like this, promise," she says to Mrs Haskins. "Thank you so much for trusting me with something so sacred. Regardless of where I end up and what I end up doing, I promise to help Amelia keep these alive. Everyone in the next generation will know them, too."

"Thank you, sugar. Now my great-great-grandma was born into slavery. Worked the fields picking cotton and tobacco."

"That's bloody awful, I'm so sorry. Some of these recipes are hers?"

Mrs Haskins nods. "And her Mama's. Recipes weren't written down since they weren't allowed to learn, so they had to commit everything to memory."

"Oh lord, that's terrible, but also fascinating that these recipes could persevere. That we're making food they were making a century and a half ago."

Mrs Haskins carefully pulls a recipe from the tin. "Let's go on and start with this one, it'll take the longest. Everyone's gonna be digging out and coming over, so the house may get a little noisy. If you need to stay in here and hideaway, no one'll give you trouble."

15

Happiness fills Remy as she stands in the cosy kitchen, surrounded by Amelia's family.

"Oh child, my bucket is overflowing. Funny enough, I always wanted to own a small cafe like Ruby's, but it was never in the cards," Mrs Haskins admits carefully wiping her hands on her full apron.

"Perhaps Ruby will let us take over her diner to do a pop-up?" Remy says without fully realising she's said it.

"Oh no, I can't ask you to stay here and do something like that for me," Mrs Haskins says, waving it away.

"Serving in a kitchen with you would be an honour, Mrs Haskins. If you believe Ruby would let us, I'll let my restaurant know I'm staying longer and blame it on the snow."

"Ruby is half tempted to sell the place to you, I'm sure she'd be willing to host a pop-up. What is that?" Amelia asks.

"Well, clearly it's something that pops up and exists for a spell. Would you need a photographer?" Rose asks.

"Oh yes! I would love to work with you, your work is so inspiring. It makes me want to turn your photos into desserts." Remy shakes her head and glances down. "Which is stupid, I'm stupid, I don't know—"

"Why you're being so mean to yourself? That's not stupid at all. I'd love to see what my photos would taste like," Rose assures her, patting Remy's shoulder.

"And you could use the family recipes, Mama, and Remy could make photo desserts and—"

"Okay, let's chat with Ruby and see her thoughts. If she's onboard, we can talk about the food you want to serve and what your place looks like in your mind. Sound good, Mrs Haskins?"

"Oh goodness, I'm honoured an award-winning chef wants to spend time in the kitchen with me. This is something I do for fun."

"You're remarkable at it, I can't wait to try everything."

"Everyone, gather around for grace, then let's see how Remy and I did."

The table is long enough everyone can sit together with the food family style down the centre. Remy sits next to Amelia, taking in the energy realising what family and holidays can look like.

"Wait, they got fancy art plates for lunch. Aren't we gettin' fancy art plates too?" one cousin asks. Remy believes his name is Byron but is having trouble remembering all the names.

"If you want one, I can certainly make you a fancy plate," Remy offers.

Mrs Johnson shakes her head. "No, that was special for us aunties, you can make your own plate, Byron. Don't go making her do extra work for you."

"But—" he starts.

She shakes her head with a parental glare. "Nope. If she makes you a fancy plate, she has to make everyone a fancy plate. Nobody got time for that with all this delicious food here."

"When Mrs Haskins and I open the pop-up, I promise to make every plate special and fancy for each of you," Remy says, as if it's for sure happening. She wants it to happen and to stay longer.

"Don't keep saying things like that, I'll make you start menu planning—" Mrs Haskins says blushing slightly.

"I would love that!" Remy responds, then tries to swallow her excitement. "If you want, not like I'm utterly over the moon at the thought of menu planning and playing with recipes."

Mrs Haskins grins and reaches over patting Remy's hand. "In that case, we have another book of recipes to talk about."

"Yes, please, I would like that very much. Thank you all for the warm welcome. This is the first Christmas Eve I've had off since I started working and the only one I can remember where I wasn't hiding in a wardrobe sobbing, so thank you." She blushes and looks down willing the emotions to go away.

"No, thank you for sharing your gift with us. Now let's say grace and honour this food."

Everything tastes good. Remy tries a bite of each dish without the voices taunting her. She does small portions of things on her approved diet instead of only having salad. "Mrs Haskins, you are quite talented. You do a beautiful job bringing out the natural flavours in this chicken, its perfectly seasoned."

"And your cornbread is inspired, sugar. Haven't had it this good since Gran was around, cornbread was her specialty."

"Thanks," Remy says, swallowing her feelings with a bite of spring greens. Remy hadn't ever tried them before, but they are delicious.

"Every Sunday is somethin' but this here? If you do a pop-up, I'm gonna be there for every meal. I'll sign over my paycheck," another cousin, Keisha maybe, says taking another large bite.

"Say Remy are you one of them fancy English people with a name like Lady Duchess Remy of the fourth house?" one of the cousin's kids asks.

"No," Remy laughs. "Well, I suppose if I were being announced? Then it's 'the honourable Rebecca Marie St. Clair Kensington, daughter of Lord Garrison Rhys Kensington the Fifth and Lady Giselle St. Clair Kensington.' My father is part of our parliament, so he was given a title but I'm not titled."

"So if you and Amelia got married would she get a fancy name too?" the same kid asks.

Amelia bursts out laughing. "The terrified expression on your face, Remzie," she leans over and squeezes Remy's hand. "No, it's just British for, 'we want our kids to seem fancy but it means nothing,' right?"

Remy nods. "Exactly," she manages now the panic is subsiding.

"I learned that from Royalty U," she says, blushing.

"Well, they got that right," Remy doesn't add, they got everything else very wrong. "I'd rather just be Remy, if it's all the same? My family isn't the best."

Amelia adds something softly in the creole they speak.

"Ooo girl, I'mma take my earrings off I ever meet them," Rose says.

Remy doesn't know how to respond. "Yes, well, thank you." She clears her throat, fidgeting with her napkin. "How is everything? Anyone need more? Mrs Haskins and I each made a Chess Pie for dessert, so save room."

"Remy made one Friday night at Ruby's that was amazing. I didn't even give her a recipe just a list of ingredients. She was on the celebrity version of the Great British Baking Challenge and does that blind bake challenge at her restaurant. I was trying to stump her. Remy'd never even heard of Chess Pie and it was as if she'd been making them her whole life. She also made noodles that made me cry. She's so talented and I'm so glad we got stuck together."

"Me too. I was so upset I couldn't make it home, but the longer I've been here the more I've realised I ended up where I needed to be. You're pretty great, Doctor Bedelia."

Amelia laughs and blushes. "Stop, you can't call me that… You're pretty great too, Remzie."

"Can we watch you on the baking show, Remy? Is it on YouTube?"

Remy's surprised when she shouldn't be that these people want to spend time with her. "Oh, erm, I'm not sure? We can see if it's available over here, if that's something you really want to do?"

"Yeah! I never met no one on TV before."

"Baby, Daddy's on the TV every day for the news."

"That's the weather, it don't count, I mean real TV," she responds with an eye roll and so much attitude.

The table erupts in laughter. "Oh, I just love you, sugar. Sure, we can watch with pie before turning the good reverend's service on."

16

Remy has had the best time with Amelia and Mrs Haskins. Ruby agreed to let them take over the diner in the evenings. She'll do her business 6-2 then they'll have it 4-10 for the pop-up. Mrs Haskins named it after her great great grandma, Haddie.

Currently, instead of playing in the kitchen she's sitting in Amelia's bedroom with her therapist on telehealth. "Well, that sounds quite terrifying, I'm so sorry Remy, are you okay?"

> She shrugs. "Amelia makes things better. The severity of it was… is, if I'm being honest… Is a lot. I'm still not sure what to do with everything I'm feeling. It's so new and different, but I'm starting to believe everything Amelia is saying. Her voice is louder than the voices telling me I'm worthless and deserve to be treated as such."

"What does she do I can incorporate into our sessions?" her therapist asks.

Remy pauses instead of giving a blanket response and actually thinks about it. "Good question." She shrugs. "But I'll sign a thing so you two can chat? I just accept she's safe and I can talk to her a bit. She doesn't want anything from me, just to spend time together."

Remy may cry, she can't sit here the entire hour sobbing.

"Remember this is a safe space and you're in control. No one is going to get upset if you release your feelings instead of swallowing them."

Remy nods slightly and grabs a tissue. "I've been a blubbering mess ever since I realised how close I came to dying."

Go on and cry, Piggy, no one cares.

Remy takes a deep breath and can hear Amelia in her ear telling the little voice to fuck off.

"Everything okay?"

Remy nods. "The taunts echoing around in my head," her voice cracks and tears trickle down her cheeks. "Amelia senses I'm spiralling and says, 'tell that little voice to fuck off, Remzie.' And adds something about whatever caused the spiral and the opposite being true." She lets the tears fall.

"Good, just take a deep breath. Want me to count?"

Remy shakes her head slightly, grabbing a tissue from the box and wiping her face. "I can hear her, she does this thing, I have something called panic attacks? That's what's happening when my arms go numb and I can't breathe. I couldn't figure out how to explain them to you, maybe I didn't mention them? They happen often, but Amelia walked me through exercises and like with the voices and taunts, her voice is louder."

"Good, I'm so glad she's been so helpful! We'll be sure to reinforce the positive resources she's given you."

"I'm not sure how to feel about everything I'm feeling, I'm not even sure I can explain what's happening. It's all new and weird and—" Remy shrugs and takes a sip of water. "But not bad, more I've seen what life can look like? It's good, I think

I'm where I need to be."

Spending time in the kitchen menu planning and experimenting with Mrs Haskins has been Remy's favourite part of this. Sometimes they spend the entire day in the kitchen. Others she isn't well enough, so they lay in her room and talk about recipes or Haddie's aesthetic. Amelia has been working behind the scenes, designing the menus, planning logistics, and some secret projects she won't talk with anyone about.

When Remy wakes up, Amelia isn't in the room, she's usually sleeping on Remy's chest or cuddled up into her back. Remy gets herself together before going down to the kitchen. She isn't prepared to see Asher and Ainsley sitting in Mama's kitchen.

"Chef! Surprise!" Ainsley says doing jazz hands. "We're here to help with Haddie's."

Remy blinks. "Ainsley, Asher? What are you—You're here, am I dreaming?"

"No! When Kona said you almost died we—" Ainsley wipes her eyes. "Sorry, I just really appreciate everything you've taught me and have so much more to learn. I value your friendship and guidance so much. Kona helped us get in touch with Amelia and flew us over so we could help with Haddie's."

"I didn't think you liked me, just tolerated me to have something impressive on your resume," Remy admits with a weak chuckle running her hand through her hair.

"No, Chef," Asher says, clearing his throat. "We both appreciate you and would be devastated if anything happened. If you don't come back to Blaze, we're going with you to your next kitchen."

Ainsley nods. "What he said."

Remy can't help it, she clears the kitchen and hugs them both. "Thank you, you're my favourite people to work with, I'm glad you're here. How are you, Mrs Haskins? Want to show them what we're working on?"

She nods. "Amelia and I have a doctor's appointment later but that will give y'all time to catch up."

Remy is a bundle of nerves for the official grand opening, but it helps to have Asher and Ainsley. The LA investors put money in, so they're all getting paid to do this and it's not coming out of Remy's trust. The soft open last night went surprisingly well, and the feedback was overall positive.

Mrs Haskins asked Remy to refer to her as Mama and when Mama is in the kitchen, everyone naturally defers to her. No one has yelled at, hit, or thrown anything at Remy. This is nice. Really nice. How kitchens can and should be.

Amelia pops her head back in. "Um, we have people lining up outside. Not family or townspeople, but strangers?"

"Is the front of the house prepared?" Remy asks.

Amelia nods. "I'll be the go between. Everyone is ready out there. Y'all ready back here?"

Mama nods. "Got all these folk back here helpin' me, I'm fine honey. Promise to stop if I need a break."

Amelia glances at Remy. "Please take care of her, and of yourself, Chef Remzie."

Remy blushes. "Promise, Doctor Bedelia."

"Chef, if I may?" Ainsley asks.

Remy nods. "Yeah, yes, please."

"Thanks for letting me be a part of this, I'm glad to be here."

"I'm glad you're here, too. This is Chef Haskins' kitchen, what she says goes."

Mama smiles and adjusts the chef's coat Remy ordered for her. "Be kind to each other and yourselves. Let's get the music going and enjoy ourselves. Thank you all, this is a dream come true."

A cousin set up an old record player in the corner and gets Sister Rosetta Thorpe going. "I'll play DJ so Amelia can focus up front, Auntie."

"Thanks sugar," Mama says.

Remy fidgets with her knives, grateful they got her luggage from the rental car when the snow melted enough to pull it from the ditch.

The ticket machine starts, typically a sound that haunts her dreams and causes her to panic. Now she's relaxed and can't wait to help Mama live her dream and share her food.

17

Everything has been going well, outside a couple of minor hiccups. Still, no one has screamed at Remy or thrown anything at her.

"Chef, I wish the kitchen was like this all the time, it's so calm," Ainsley says from where she's working on sauces.

"Same, I didn't know it could be—nice," Remy responds with a smile, putting the finishing touches on a piece of Chess Pie. "Chef Haskins, are you doing okay? Need another break?"

Mama shakes her head, sitting in a chair fanning herself. "No, I'm fine sugar, a little tired. This differs from cookin' in my kitchen."

"Take your time, have some water, we've got this," Remy assures her.

Amelia comes back with a scheming smirk. "Chef Remzie, a special guest wants to say hi,"

Remy's brows go up. "Me?"

The smirk widens causing Amelia's eyes to sparkle in the kitchen lights. "Trust me, you want to come say hi,"

Remy nods. "Erm, okay, this is for table ten," she says, handing the pie plate to Amelia.

Remy walks out of the small kitchen and stops, shocked, Kona is sitting at a table. Wearing Remy's favourite red dress, hair done, enough makeup to accentuate everything good about her. Holding a massive bouquet of beautiful flowers.

"Kona? What—how—" Remy shakes her head and takes a deep breath. "Hi,"

Kona stands and hugs Remy, kissing her. "Hi, I've missed you," she murmurs against Remy's lips.

"I didn't even think you really liked me," Remy admits blushing.

Kona kisses her again. Remy didn't realise how much she missed kissing Kona until this moment. She flashes an endearing shy smile. "Amelia is the best, she helped me plan this and keep it a surprise."

Remy nods. "Yeah she is, she'll be a lifelong friend. I kissed her, but we didn't do more than kiss." Unsure why she needs to tell Kona outside she doesn't want to hurt her.

Kona chuckles. "Kiss and date whomever you want. I just want to spend whatever time together we can."

Remy blushes and clears her throat. "No one has ever bought me flowers, or flown thousands of kilometres. Can I make you something?"

Kona kisses her again and Remy's stomach flutters. "Perhaps a few things off the menu," she whispers with a wink and eyebrow waggle. "Amelia helped me order, we talked before I asked her to get you."

"Uh oh, why does that feel serious?" Remy asks, stomach and throat clenching.

Kona waves the fear away. "No, no, I wanted to make sure I wasn't crossing any boundaries."

"When we first met I was ready to shag it out, but I don't want that anymore. Only to cuddle, talk, and be friends."

"How about me?" Kona asks, vulnerability softening her striking features. "Would you be open to spending more time together? Possibly using the g or p-word?"

Remy nods, as terrifying as the thought is. "If you really want to?"

Kona laughs. "Oh chicken, I flew thousands of kilometres and brought flowers. Yes, I genuinely like you, but only an appropriate amount."

Remy bites her lip to keep from crying and turns to run away from the feelings welling up. "I really must get back to the kitchen."

Mama is at the counter refilling her water. "Nah, we're fine sugar, go on and sit with your girl." She looks at Kona. "I'm Mrs Haskins, I look forward to getting to know you better, Kona. That dress is stunning on you."

"Isn't it? Every time she wears it I forget myself," Remy hears herself saying.

Kona blushes. "That's why I wore it." She glances up at Mama. "Same, thank you Mrs Haskins, I can't wait to try the food," Kona responds.

Remy sits with Kona. "I shouldn't be sitting during service…" before she can panic Amelia's voice chases away the taunting voices in her head.

"Are you going to tell Chef Haskins no?" Kona asks.

Remy shakes her head with a chuckle. "No, she's in charge. If she wants me to sit, I'll sit. She's been helpful for me, she and Amelia both." Remy inspects the flowers. "These are lovely. Where did you find flowers around here?"

"Actually, I picked them up on my layover," she says blushing and glancing down. "Figured if I'm flying around the world to ask you to be my partner I needed to pull out all the stops."

Remy kisses her. "Thank you, it's fantastic to see you. I hadn't realised how much I've missed you until you were standing here. Sorry for being me and maybe not doing the best job of making time for you or telling you, you matter."

"Don't be too hard on yourself, you did when and what you could, I knew what I was signing up for when we met, MiMi."

Remy blushes. "You can't call me that here, I'm at work."

Kona leans in hot breath tickling Remy's neck. "I'll call you so many things when we're alone, if you'll consent?"

Remy can't say anything, just smiles and nods blushing. "Yeah, I'd like that." She clears her throat, taking Kona's hand and squeezing. "Tomorrow I can make brunch at Mama's?"

Kona nods and shifts so she can curl into Remy. "I love when you cook for me."

"Good, all right, I um, how are you, how's work?"

Kona laughs. "Good, I'm just working on the next book in the series, my agent and editor are impatiently patiently waiting."

Kona does truly magnificent things with words. Remy has never found an author that engages her the way Kona and her worlds do. "Which series the dragons or the coffeeshop?"

"Dragons—" tears well up, Kona blinks them back. "I didn't think you knew my work."

"Oh, I've read everything you've published, KoKo, or listened to at the gym," Remy responds with a warm smile, leaning in to kiss Kona.

Amelia slides into the booth with two plates and sets them down with coffee for Remi and wine for Kona. "Mama made something special, Kona, a welcome meal. You're important to Remy, so you're important to us."

Kona blushes and sputters slightly. "A proper amount. Please don't run!"

Remy is panicking and wants to run, instead she hugs Kona tighter and kisses her forehead. "Same, a proper amount. Thanks for this, Doctor Bedelia, I appreciate you."

Amelia stands giggling. "Oh you two, alright, enjoy your time then whenever you have a moment they need you back in the kitchen, Chef Remzie. No rush, and everyone means that, in case that voice is kicking around."

The panic immediately dissipates and Remy nods, taking a deep breath and pushing it out.

Kona shifts up, kissing Remy. "I think this is the longest we've been together with our clothes on. We need to do this more."

"Same, not that being naked is awful, but I'd like to go on a proper date with you," Remy says, smiling. She gestures to the food. "This recipe is from the late eighteen-hundreds, we made it for the first time a few days ago. I love all these old recipes."

"Perhaps we can break out my Nene's cookbook sometime and play in the kitchen?" Kona says biting her lip slightly.

"Yes, I'd love that!" Remy clears her throat and blushes. "Sorry, just the right amount, sounds wonderful, I didn't know you cook."

"Obviously, your way better at it, but I dabble."

"Let's dabble together. Can I read what you're working on? I want to see what's happening with Neville and Nan, they're my favourite characters of yours."

Kona blinks away tears and nods. "I rarely let people read things before they're edited, but I trust you."

"Take a bite, tell me what you think."

Kona obliges, taking a small bite and her face melts. "Oh wow, did you make this?"

Remy shakes her head. "That's all Mama, isn't she incredible?"

"A natural, I would've put money down that's yours. Try a bite." She holds the fork up for Remy.

Instead of panicking, Remy leans forward and takes the bite. "Oh, yeah, she outdid herself, that slaps, as Amelia's cousins say."

Kona giggles and takes the pen from behind her ear

writing something on the napkin. Which Remy has noticed she does when she wants to remember something for a story.

"Am I inspiring storylines?"

"Chef!" Ainsley hollers from the kitchen.

Remy wants to jump up and run but doesn't want to be rude.

Kona winks and kisses her. "Go on back to the kitchen, I'll be here whenever you're done."

18

The team fell into a comfortable routine at Haddie's with things running effortlessly. Amelia handled the front of the house with Auntie Tamika. Kona was there every night from open to close, working on her next book. Remy enjoyed making little tasting plates for her to snack on while she worked and finding moments to say hi and steal a kiss.

Mama does less cooking and more directing from a chair, which is worrisome. Remy doesn't want anything happening to her.

The reviews have all been positive, which almost never happens.

It's Friday night, and there's a line wrapped around the building. Organised chaos envelops the kitchen as everyone dances around each other. Kona comes back with her bag and plate. "I gave my seat up. Mind if I hang out back here? Promise to stay out of the way."

"Sure sugar, come sit with me, you can help fetch things for me. I'm feeling the uninvited guest today."

Remy loves when Mama refers to her cancer as an uninvited guest, it makes it a little less terrifying.

"Anything, Mama," Kona responds with a warm smile.

Mama insisted since Kona was important to Remy she was family and had to stop calling her ma'am or Mrs Haskins.

Amelia sneaks back and kisses Remy, then Kona, and hugs Mama. "Heard you might need a lie down. Can I get you anything?"

"You're not here to check up on me, you just wanted to snog your lady friends," Mama says with a twinkle in her eye.

It's been nice to kiss and cuddle with Kona and Amelia. The three of them end up asleep on the couch most nights. Everyone is accepting enough. Mama put to rest anything too bad by threatening folks with no longer having a seat at Sunday dinner and missing out on the amazing food they create together.

"Mama," Amelia says, blushing.

Remy chuckles. How has it only been six weeks since seeing Amelia blush for the first time?

She and Kona are taking things slow, not allowing Remy to use any of her terrible coping mechanisms, which is both nice and not. She's had more telehealth appointments with her therapist, seeing her three times a week. Which has both been awful and helpful. Amelia helps. Kona helps. This kitchen helps.

"Cousin, there's someone with a whole camera crew outside they want to do interviews?" Rose says, leaning into the kitchen.

"I'll handle it," Amelia says, heading back out with a little wink at Kona and eyebrow waggle at Remy.

"This has turned into quite something. Perhaps we should make it more permanent?" Asher says to no one in particular.

"Count me in. I can't go back to toxic kitchens now I've seen what it can be like," Ainsley adds from where she's finishing a plate.

"I can't go back either, they offered to bring us to LA, or we can take Ruby up on her offer to sell us this place? Get a place back home…"

"Lots to think about, sugar. Keisha, be a dear and help me over to Ruby's will you?"

Remy shifts from what she's doing to what Keisha's doing so the cousin can help Mama back to the house.

"Wherever you are, Chef. I just want to keep cooking with you," Asher says.

"Same," Ainsley confirms.

"What about you, Kona? Any thoughts?"

She blushes and blinks back tears. "I told you I can be a writer anywhere, MiMi—I mean Chef."

Amelia comes back into the kitchen. "Can you and Mama come out?" she asks.

"Mama went for a lie down, we're a little shorthanded, but I suppose I can, if it won't take long?"

Amelia nods. "It'll only be a moment."

Remy walks out with Amelia and it's not just any camera team, they're from the most exclusive food programme in the UK.

"Chef Kensington, thank you for taking time out for us!" Francis, the host says with a warm smile.

"Francis, wonderful to see you again. What brings you here?" Remy asks, kissing her on either cheek.

Francis laughs. "You Chef and the remarkable flavours you're putting out in this small town diner. The food and flavours are truly inspiring. How did you come up with the menu?"

Remy shrugs and slides her hands into her pockets to keep from fidgeting. "This started playing in the kitchen during the blizzard over the holiday. Chef Haskins mentioned she'd always wanted to have a modest place to share her family's recipes, so I offered to help make that happen."

"What's the secret to the Tearful Noodles? I've never seen

so many people reduced to tears by a dish before. It's sweeping social media."

"Can I tell this story?" Amelia asks. "You'll downplay it," she glances at Francis. "Chef Kensington always downplays her talent."

"Sure," Francis says with a subtle wink at Remy.

"We were snowed in here at the diner together during the blizzard and to stave off the panic Chef Kensington cooked. She was trying to avoid a conversation where I was praising her talent and shifted her focus to throwing this noodle dish together. Look at the plates she made! Mind you this is when it was just a diner feeding a small town." Amelia holds up the picture of the plates.

Francis gasps. "Those are beautiful. You made those here before this was Haddie's?"

"Yes!" Amelia exclaims. "The first bite reduced me to tears and the rest is history."

"It's just something I threw together," Remy says blushing and glancing down, fidgeting with the snap on her sleeve before shifting her hands back to her pockets.

"And the famous Chess Pie was also something that came out of your snowcation?" Francis asks.

"Yes! I didn't even give Chef a recipe, just a list of ingredients. She is so talented, savoury and sweet, she can do it all."

"Well, we won't keep you any longer, Chef Kensington. Oh! Congratulations on your star. How does it feel?"

"We earned a star?" Remy asks quietly. She can't make a fool of herself by crying on the telly.

Mama comes out from the back holding an envelope with a small smile. "Can you read it? I can't seem to find my glasses."

Remy takes a deep breath and blinks back her tears. "Oh, wow, we won a star—" she takes another deep breath. "I only wanted to help Chef Haskins share food that has existed in the heads and hearts of her family for generations. Sorry, excuse me, I need to get back to the kitchen, the food won't make itself."

Remy gets to the cooler before she breaks and starts sobbing.

Kona quietly pushes in and hugs her. Remy fists her shirt and allows herself to fall to pieces for a moment before pulling back together.

"We got a star, KoKo," she says with a choppy breath.

"Oh, that's wonderful!"

Remy hugs Kona a little tighter and takes a deep breath in slowly pushing it out.

"Can we celebrate later?"

Kona nods. "And we can celebrate my news too? Starz wants to give me ridiculous amounts of money to adapt Dragons into a series."

"You've always wanted that! Congrats!" Remy is rarely so expressive, but this warrants speaking in exclamation marks.

"I'll duck out and get us a bottle of champagne we can celebrate together," Kona says. "Unless you want to hide and hug more?"

Remy nods. "But I need to get back out there."

She and Kona walk out of the cooler together. "We earned a star!" Remy says, doing her level best not to dissolve into tears again.

Everyone else in the kitchen mirrors her excitement and shock.

"I bet this is only the beginning for us, sugar," Mama says with a tired smile. "Help me back to bed."

Remy nods and she and Mama casually walk back over to Ruby's house.

"I am so proud of us. Thank you for making my dream a reality. This has been wonderful."

"Me too, thank you for this."

"Just because my time runs out doesn't mean it runs out for you. The recipes are Amelia and Lane's, but I want you to help them. Even wrote it into my will that the recipes and Haddie's, that you're a part of it too. All I ask is you help keep the recipes alive and don't let anyone steal them or give them away. They are our families and they're meant for us. That's what makes them special. Share the food, but we must protect where the food comes from."

Remy nods. "Yes, of course, you have my word."

"Good. I love you and I am so proud of you, Remy," Mama says with a little cough, lying down on the bed in the guest room.

"I love you too, Mama," Remy says, and means it, she genuinely loves this woman.

"Go on back to the kitchen while I rest."

Remy nods and hugs Mama tightly before walking back over to the kitchen.

"I'm going to go sit with Mama for a minute," Amelia says. "Something doesn't feel right."

Remy nods. "Sounds good, I like and appreciate you, Doctor Bedilia."

"I like and appreciate you too, Chef Remzie."

Remy gets back into the groove doing what she loves surrounded by people she cares about. The blizzard landed her where she was meant to be, and she recognises this is just the beginning. Things will only get better from here.

Thank you for reading!

If you can spare a minute and leave a review that's incredibly helpful for indie authors.

Other works from Shannon Massey:

Welcome To The Resistance, a horrifying political thriller set in a reality that closely mirrors our own. Former Speaker of the House, Lily VonHelm, leads a resistance against the tyrannical dictator that stole the 2016 US presidential election and plunged the United States into a fascist nightmare.

Partner In Wine: (sapphic drama) Alzheimer's patient Marjory Farmington Shire escapes her memory care facility and embarks on an adventure to reunite with her wife and children for the holidays. The only problem? She believes it's 1975.

Above and Beyond (sapphic sci-fi) Political prisoner, M'Awk, crash lands on an alien planet in quarantined space after attempting to escape a prison transport and her sadistic guards. Sally is the lonely Alaskan park ranger that stumbles upon the wreckage.

Whiskey Rivers: Far Space (queer sci-fi horror) Captain Chakrum Gravers is a 3rd Gen spacer with an old mining ship, Whiskey Rivers, and a small crew. Things get complicated when they find an asteroid with more than just minerals in it.

Andi's Livestream: Apocalypse Edition (sapphic sci-fi rom-com) Andi has a massive crush on her best friend Adair, and she's finally going to say something today during her livestream. She has everything planned and even wrote a script with all the various possibilities. Well, almost all of them. She didn't anticipate an alien invasion interrupting her livestream. Can Andi survive long enough to profess her love?

Published in:

Black Rainbow: Queer horror anthology
Maleficence: An anthology of queer disabled villainy

Milton Keynes UK
Ingram Content Group UK Ltd.
UKHW041321041224
452078UK00012B/2